PAREIDOLIA

SHRISHTI VENKATRAMAN

ISBN 979-8-89133-683-4

I give thanks for the ordinary

For days that start with a perfect coffee

And end with a bright smile

When nothing awaits me, when I await nothing

Dear Reader,

I'd like to start by expressing my immense gratitude that you have chosen to read this book. You have generously devoted your time and attention, which is more than I could ever ask for. I hope that by the end of this book, I manage to bring at least one percent of the happiness that my favourite authors bring to me.

When I began writing this book, I didn't have a precise idea of what I expected it to become. Honestly, even now, if you were to ask me to describe it in a single word, I would be searching for the perfect answer. To me, this book embodies joy and grief, sweetness and sourness, love and loss. It's filled with the musings that wander in my head, stories I've felt compelled to narrate, and poetry into which I've poured my heart. I don't know if this is what you were seeking when you wanted a book to read, but writing this book has unquestionably been one of the most fulfilling experiences of my life.

I'm one of those teenagers who are still figuring things out, in contrast to some of my classmates who already have their entire futures planned out. Three things that have consistently helped calm my nerves for as long as I can remember are writing, reading, and painting.

This book is an amalgamation of the mundane thoughts in my head. It's a piece of me displayed for you. It's a collection of the most random things you'll read—some are important stories, while others are just figments of my wild imagination. I've always sought to find magic in the mundane, so some parts of this book are about me discovering the simple joys of life amidst all the humdrum and complaining.

I've always believed that imagination is the master of all sins. What would you say if I told you to imagine a psychopath in love? And what would you imagine if I asked you to consider that, to me, up and down, right and wrong feel the same? This book is as random as that one thought, so I hope you understand what you've signed up for.

It's a blend of all things ordinary—events that occur every day—and a few things I wish happened every day. "Pareidolia" is a word that literally means the tendency to perceive meaningful things in ambiguous ways. It's the human ability to make sense out of randomness. Therefore, to me, it's the perfect name for a compilation of the aimless thoughts in my head.

Love and regards,

Shrishti

CONTENTS

1

THE ORDINARY

As I peer through my bedroom window, staring at two kids playing on the road under the scorching sun, my mind wonders what stories they hide inside those tiny bodies. I keep staring at the kids, at the sky, at a stray dog limping around looking for food, and just like that, my mind returns to my room. My diary in my hand, I resume reading through it.

I realise that I talk a lot about bad days, ruined projects, mean people, and the cruelties of fate. I fill pages about how much kinder life could've been to me. I keep talking about how everyone but me has lives so colourful and interesting. I skim through a few more pages to realise that I've written a few nice things too. I've written about how I met a nice person, did a nice thing, went on a family outing, listened to Taylor Swift's new album, and had random conversations with my best friend. My mouth curves up in a smile, but I also realise that there is no place in my diary for a seemingly ordinary day.

A day just like other days, a day where I wake up, do what I must do, and sleep. But why would I? Ordinary days just stack up one after the other. They mean hardly anything. I could fill in the same entry during my summer and winter vacation. Ordinary days aren't characterised by pent-up emotions, deadlines to meet, tests to study for, and new lessons learned. Neither are they days when my heart swells up with warmth, when I'm overcome by a sense of joy and love. They're just ordinary.

There are no big wins or terrible failures. No new friends are made, no interesting conversations happen, no annoying person in the picture, and no headline gossip talked about.

No fights with people you love, no apologies made after swallowing one's pride. If I started talking about ordinary days, wouldn't my diary become like one of those books that seem to stand still? Where the future of the protagonist is ever so confusing? A book you read just for the heck of finishing it. A book with no plot twists. A book where no scene makes you gasp out loud.

Yet, as I sip on the cup of tea my mother just gave me, I revel in how perfect it tastes. When I feel the summer breeze tangling my hair, see those two kids pulling each other's hair but eventually making up after their fight, and my eyes find the dog nibbling on a piece of flesh while I hear the pitter-patter of rain, the most unexpected thing on a hot summer afternoon, I feel at peace.

When you smile at a random person on the street, and they smile back. When you don't burn your morning toast. When you feel wholesome after reading a perfectly well-written book. When you help an old woman cross the street. When life decides to just let you be. When you feel grateful for the number of people God put in your life to always have your back. It's ordinary, but it's beautiful.

Ordinary days provide a much-needed balance for all our emotions. The little things that happen on these days add up to something huge. So, every time you start complaining about how monotonous a day is, remember that on days like these, dreaming and hoping come easily.

And so, I reach for my pen, bite the cap off (since my free hand is holding the teacup), and I start writing. I tell my diary about the silly joke my brother cracked today. I talk about the old couple I saw in the mall. I ramble on about the mindless arguments I had with a bazillion different people. I talk about the two kids and the dog on the road. I write about how thankful I am that tea and coffee exist. I write about how I had a random urge to break something today. About how music is one of the best things to ever exist. About how I thought of someone from my old school out of nowhere. I tell my diary about how I want to reconnect with that one friend, about the twenty eight different imaginary conversations I had in my head. With a smile plastered on my face, I write about how I quoted a One Direction lyric in my English answer sheet. I write about how offended I was when the delivery guy assumed I'm twenty years old. I continue to express how much the sound of raindrops falling on the ground calms my nerves.

About the eyes of a stranger I saw on the road today, I write about how frustrated I'll be when the weekend slips away and Monday arrives like a funeral.

And just like that, I end up filling quite a few pages. I make it a point to write in my diary even on days when life feels pointless.

"There's a lot of beauty in ordinary things,
isn't that kind of the point?

2

I Killed Someone

The blaring sound of my phone ringing worsens my headache. I scratch my red eyes, gently caressing the heavy bags beneath them, and reach for my phone on the bedside table to switch off the alarm. In doing so, I even managed to knock over a glass of water on the table. Good morning indeed.

I tie my hair up in a bun, spray some cologne on my body, grab my keys, and head out. I descend the stairs, and just as I'm about to open my car door, I slip on a banana peel. I fall with a thud, and the contents of my heavy and messy handbag are scattered all over the basement floor. As if it couldn't get any worse. I don't give myself any more time to wallow in self-pity. With all the strength I can muster, I pick up my things from the floor and get into the car. As soon as I settle into the seat, I hear a grumbling sound. Considering I had leftovers for dinner yesterday and no breakfast today, I wasn't surprised. But I didn't have time. I overslept, and my mind is already thinking of 13 different excuses that will convince the hospital authorities otherwise.

I roll down the car windows; the AC was making me nauseous, and my headache wasn't helping. As I lower the windows, I see my neighbour Sasha laughing with her two-year-old son, taking him to his first day of school. She is a housewife, modest and happy. I've wondered many times if I'd swap my life for hers. She lives a simple life, stays in the apartment all day, takes care of her family, and helps organise community events. As enticing as it sounds, I know that kind of life would never satisfy me; simple has never been enough in my dictionary.

The blaring horns on the highway make my head throb with frustration. The hospital is ten kilometres away, and I should've been there half an hour ago. With the traffic congestion I see clogging the roads, I highly doubt I'll reach on time.

While I wait for the signal to turn green, I hear my phone ringing. It's from one of the nurses who assists me. She is most likely calling to inform me how late I am, as if I don't already know. I ignore the first call, but when she decides to call 3 more times, I don't really have a choice. I pick it up.

"Ma'am, are you there?" she asks, in a voice laced with anxiety.

"Yes, Priya, I'll reach the hospital in a while. What is it?" I reply, frustrated for no valid reason.

"The patient who got admitted last week, the one with a high fever and a running nose, the eight-year-old kid, he's been screaming in pain for a while now. I don't know what to do."

I mutter a string of curses under my breath. That kid annoyed me the second he got admitted; he's always in pain.

"Give him a painkiller or two," I reply absentmindedly.

She replies with a meek, confused "yes," and I hang up.

I ask myself what I've become. Years of hardly any sleep, late nights studying in my dorm room when my friends were out partying, and midnight surgeries. I haven't called my parents in weeks. In fact, I cannot remember the last time I did anything that wasn't associated with my career.

Somehow lost in these thoughts, I manage to reach the hospital. I show the guard my ID and head to my office. But I'm stopped midway by a higher authority. She's never been too fond of me. Her black eyes pierce right into me from her thick round glasses. Streaks of her grey hair fall on her slumped shoulders.

She looks tired, but there's a fire in her eyes, one that's never doused. She knows the implications of her job, and yet her passion drives her.

"Good morning. Can I help you, ma'am?" I ask her in a raspy voice.

"Did you ask Priya to give one of your patients painkillers? Did you confirm with her why he was feeling pain? Did you ask her anything regarding his condition before ordering her to give him those pills?"

Typical of her to cut to the chase, I think to myself. But fear engulfs me when I see her prying eyes searching my face, her disappointment in me visibly spread across her face.

I cannot bring myself to say anything. My throat is suddenly drier than usual. Tears threaten to spill from my eyes. I find myself nodding a minute later.

"He's in the ICU. His chances of survival are low. We need to conduct surgery within the next two hours. Put on your scrubs and gloves and be there in 15 minutes," she commands in the most clipped tone ever. Lines of worry furrow on her forehead, and I realise I've messed up.

I place my bag at the reception, grab my coat, and rush to the ICU room. My hands are trembling, and I feel my lips quiver. Guilt gushes over me. It is taking everything in me to hold myself together. As I wait for my colleagues to join me in the room, my mind drifts back to medical school.

I was 18; it was my first day of college. I remember my professor came up to me and said he saw passion in my eyes. From that day on, I tried my best to carry that passion and vigour with me for the following years. And somehow, between late-night duty calls and instant food breakfasts, I lost it.

You see, they taught us everything in college, everything in theory. But no one told me what I must do when someone is on their deathbed because of me. No one taught me how to deal with the million different obstacles life will throw at me. No one taught me what I must do if I just stopped caring.

And so here I am, waiting with bated breath. I always knew this is what I signed up for. Even if I did manage to forget, I had tons of people who'd tell me every day that I hold the lives of people in the palm of my hand. And yet, when for the first time in the two years of my rather successful career, I make a mistake, I'm not able to handle the torment and the grief. Tears welling up in my eyes blur my vision, but I wipe them off when I hear my colleagues approaching.

We entered the room. I picked up my tools with shaking hands and performed the surgery on the man, a young man in his late twenties. I pretended as though his age didn't affect me. I pretended as though his condition wasn't my fault. I blamed it on fate. I told myself that what was meant to be would be. And just like that, I finished the surgery.

Everyone in the room turned to the heart rate monitor. It flickered for a while, and in a matter of what felt like hours but was probably just minutes, it stilled into a straight line.

He's dead.

I killed him.

I robbed a mother of the son she'd nurtured.

I robbed a father of the son he'd loved.

I robbed the world of a human life.

I drop the tools and rush out of the room. I sit on one of the hospital benches. When I try to collect myself, I see two elders approaching me—elders with seemingly similar physical features to the man I just murdered: his parents.

They approach me, travelling from another state upon hearing their son was in danger. They ask me if he's alright, if he'll live. I stifle sobs and, with the calmest voice I can muster, tell them their son is no more. I see his mother falling apart in front of me, his father trying to stay composed to console his wife, although I know he's breaking apart on the inside too. I witness their tears and violent sobs.

My breathing intensifies, and my head spins. I cannot think or see straight. The voices around me are muffled. With every ounce of strength in me, I go to the balcony. I hold onto the railing to prevent myself from tripping. I try to inhale as much air as I can. After what feels like an eternity, I regain my stability.

I shudder when I feel someone touch my shoulder. I quickly turn and see the last person I expected: the senior official who despises the sight of me, trying to console me. Her hands move up and down the length of my shoulder, comforting me. She whispers sweet nothings into my ear as she hugs me. She tells me about the first time she failed in a surgery and someone died. She explains how it shattered her, but over the years, she got used to it. I know she intends to comfort me, but the fact that I need to become accustomed to the idea of causing people's deaths in my future career terrifies me.

My eyes are red and streaming with hot tears. She knows her efforts to comfort me are in vain, but she persists. She tells me I'm no robot, she emphasises that all humans make mistakes. She talks about how this job drains everyone in the hospital, yet they continue to persevere. When I finally manage to utter something that isn't just incoherent whispers, I raspily convey that I will never be able to get over how I took someone's life.

She responds, "At least the next time a nurse calls you with a similar problem, you'll be more careful."

She imparts a few more soothing words in her gentle voice. I finally wipe away my tears. I don't think I can move on from something so significant. It will take me weeks, if not months.

But it's inevitable. What happened today is a lesson for the future, and it might take me a long time to fully accept that, but I will. I'll make sure to do my best to avoid repeating something like this.

I hear a grumbling noise, and for once, it's not my stomach; it's hers. We both grab something from the cafeteria and get back to work.

3

THE BOY I KNEW

There was a boy I knew
Hazel skin, pitch-black eyes
A face so beautiful
He looked like an angel

One who'd just descended from the blue sky
What's his name, you ask?
I wouldn't know

In fact, I doubt he knows his own name

And when you finally manage to stop looking
Into his beautiful eyes
You see the gun in his hand
He walks deserted streets holding the gun
Where did he learn to use it, you ask?
I wouldn't know but I imagine
He learned it as a child
When you and I learned to walk and speak.
Or maybe it comes naturally to him.
And so this boy

He walks on his two small feet
To the local firing at the park
Where kids his age play on swings
He pulls the trigger.

He wipes the red off his face

But ends up smearing it across his lips instead
Why, you ask?
I don't know and I imagine he wouldn't either
He doesn't know.
He was born in a country driven by war
A country where war is the way of life

Children watch their parents get killed
Parents kill to prevent their children from dying
Every day someone dies
A mother, a brother, a teacher.
And so this little boy
Watches as hundreds get killed

While also constantly pulling the trigger.
And when it's all over
When they're all gone

He lays down on the wet garden grass.
He yearns to feel,
But he finds himself incapable of anything but murder
He notices a couple walking towards him
And so, he gets up

Every cell in his body wants to beg them to leave
But instead he pulls the trigger
A storm in his gut, his heart so heavy
Suddenly another bullet leaves another gun
But it's not his this time
He falls to the ground

His eyes idly stare at the sky

He hopes he'll finds his way back
Somewhere among those clouds

4

TENTH GRADE: THE RANT

I stare up at the wall clock, the bags under my eyes begging me to go to bed. It's 1 a.m., and I've been sitting here all night, gazing at my history book, trying to memorise those 25 pages about the Russian and French revolutions.

My brother emerges from the bedroom to get a drink of water.

"You need to sleep; we have school tomorrow!" he says. My brother offering me advice only makes my headache worse.

"Besides, it's social studies. You can babble and still get marks," he adds. "You know, if zombies ever took over, you'd be safe," I say out of the blue. Confused, he asks, "Why?"

"They only eat brains. You clearly don't have one." It might have been a stupid thing to say, but my brain hasn't been functioning well past twelve.

"You're upset," he sighs. "And you're a genius!" I retort. "Now go back to sleep."

After almost two years of doing this, staying up past midnight doesn't seem like too tough a task.

But I've had my phases. It started when I entered ninth grade. Family members warned me about what was to come, how important these years of my life would be, and how these results matter so much. They told me that if I worked hard enough during these few years, the rest of my life would sail smoothly. The daily tests scared me, and the mammoth portions for each of them terrified me. But like every other one of my classmates, I got used to it. I became accustomed to staying up every day, preparing for a new exam every night.

Then slowly, it all just became normal; it became a part of me. I stopped complaining and just went with whatever happened. Sometimes I'd turn up to tests not as prepared as I usually prided myself on being, and sometimes my grades slipped. But you couldn't expect anyone to consistently score well for all of two years.

Then, during the last few months of tenth grade, I just couldn't wait to get it over with. The bottled-up frustration started pouring out and how. Sometimes I'd start throwing things around, getting angry for no reason, shouting at my brother, and talking back to my parents as if it would somehow make the annoying feeling go away. The space station probably could hear me grinding my teeth in frustration all the way into outer space.

And then finally came that one Sunday evening; it was all finally going to be over. Of course, it was just the first exam, with four more to go. But I'd heard everyone say that after the first one, it all happens quickly. I brace myself for my English exam, one of the 5 that apparently would shape my future and decide what I will become, the person I'd be. I couldn't sleep that night. I remember re-reading the same old chapters a hundred times, checking if I missed something I'd regret not learning in the exam the next day. I kicked my feet, turned left and right, chanted slokas, but sleep just wouldn't pay me a visit that night. But somehow, between hallucinating the hundred different ways tomorrow could go wrong and revising word meanings in my head, I fell asleep.

The next morning, I woke up as soon as I could. I grabbed my bag and checked a hundred times if I had my hall ticket, pens, and pencils. I prayed to God as I stepped out of the house.

"Just breathe," I hear my mother telling me. "I am," I reply.

"You're hyperventilating."

"It's a normal response to abnormal situations!" I groan.

"It's just English; there's only so much that could go wrong. We've been doing it all year," I tell myself a million times.

Finally, I reach the exam hall and head to the waiting room, where I find all my friends, each in a different headspace. Some are just as anxious as I am, while others are a little less so. And, of course, there's that gang, unbothered and completely ignorant. It's not like they didn't study; they just couldn't care less. They weren't scared; they'd do their best and leave the rest to fate. If only I could be that composed! And then there's me, walking around under a black cloud of nervousness so thick, it has its own atmosphere.

I make my way to my best friend, and we revise the few things we can. All my classmates gather around; we wish each other luck and say a group prayer. Then we enter those dreaded exam halls. There is nothing tenser than the air before those papers are distributed. The examiner looks around, walks up and down the length of the hall, while my hands and legs shake out of nervousness.

The question paper reaches my hands after what seems like hours' worth of waiting. I tense up when I read through it for the first time, suddenly feeling as though my brain has gone blank, like I don't know anything. The second time, I'm a little more confident; I know most of it. I can do it.

You know the one thing slightly more frustrating than waiting for your paper? Filling up the OMR sheets, making sure you don't shade the wrong circle or shade outside of the circle.

And then three hours pass as quickly as they can, and we hand in our papers. You can feel our relief in the air, our sighs, and exclamations of joy. We're done with these English textbooks we've been carrying around all these months.

1 down, four to go. On a scale of one to ten, my frustration is probably fifty-eight. But we'll get through this, I tell myself.

And just like days pass, weeks go by, and finally, it's the last exam.

MATH.

After numerous exhausting late nights spent studying, this was it. And, of course, they saved the worst for last. There's not much revising you can do with math, but we still repeated those same 20 formulae as many times as we could.

And just like that, those 3 hours also passed.

We handed over our papers. It's finally over. The relief that visibly washed over our faces could not be missed by even the most ignorant observer. After two years of preparing for these exams and exhausting ourselves with revising the same things numerous times, we're finally done with tenth grade.

But apparently, that wasn't the end. We have two months of waiting for the results. And a multitude of people asking us how we did. I've never found the right answer to that one question. I think I did well, but is that enough? I wouldn't know; I've never been confident enough to come out of an exam hall saying I did extremely well. Anything could go wrong, page numbers, question numbers, dates, and equations. So many things you can mess up.

I'm still waiting. Sometimes I can't sleep at night even now, thinking about my results. Whether I'll be okay with anything.

But I genuinely hope that when I grow up, and I'm sitting on my couch going through old diaries or reminiscing memories, I don't think of the studying and the results when I think of tenth grade.

I hope I think of the laughs we shared between classes. I hope I smile when I think of the hundred million methods of cheating during tests we came up with. I hope I think of my teachers and all they've done. I hope I still laugh at the inside jokes of the class. I hope I think of how wholesome the farewell was. I hope I think of how we'd all turn up with the most diverse lunches and share food and loud laughs during lunch break.

I hope I think of all the things that made this year so much better than it would have been if I hadn't been surrounded by the loudest laughs, the funniest jokes, and the silliest dramas in the world.

For isn't that what makes life, life? To have loved and to have lost. To have laughed our hearts out. To have people you look back at and smile about. To remember that one overdramatic classmate or that one extremely quiet classmate. To hold onto that one best friend forever because you never let go of people like that. To come home and tell your mother twenty-five funny things that happened that day.

I let out a sigh as I think about what the future holds for me; right now, it is only a blob of nothingness. A blank canvas waiting for me to splash bright, beautiful colours on it as I take one more step closer to what will ultimately become of me.

The one thing I know for sure is that right now life's pretty good, and it might not be the same way after a while, but I'll enjoy it while it lasts.

And so, here I am writing random stories, painting mundane things, slowly filling up my huge blank canvas. We're all navigating life in our own beautiful ways because what good is a planned and strategised life if you're not happy with the end goal, with what has already been decided for you.

5

THE MYSTERY GIRL

As I brush past the scrawly, illegible handwriting my ten-year-old self could manage to jot down in her diary, I come across this one entry on one of those hot April evenings. It was summer vacation, and I'm used to spending those at my grandmother's place. The taste of her lip-smacking food still lingers somewhere at the tip of my tongue, the aroma reaching every room from the kitchen, the comfort of her embrace, and how my cousins and I would huddle up to listen to her narrating stories of the past.

I recall that one April evening to this day; it was hot and humid. To add to our discomfort, the power had been cut off. It was around 7 or 8 in the evening, I think, and none of us could see anything, our eyes shrouded by pitch-black darkness. My grandmother somehow made her way to the kitchen and lit up one of those thick white candles and brought it to the living room.

We all scooted next to her and clung to her saree. During these times, when we're all covered in sweat and afraid of the dark, my grandmother would tell us stories, stories about her past or myths that have been passed on from one generation to another. And today was no different, except I felt like I saw a glimmer of a different emotion in her eyes. Sadness, maybe? I wouldn't know, or maybe it was just a figment of my own silly, wandering imagination.

That evening, we were lucky enough to hear something that had happened to her. She started off in her hoarse voice and told us about her village.

She used to live in a small little hut with her 9 sisters, a brother, and her parents. She told us about their fights and apologies, how they'd all finish with all household chores and rush to school. She told us with a gleam in her eyes about the pranks they'd play, the way they'd sneak out of their house, and when caught, they'd be given a piece of their parents' minds. She then told us about this one friend she once had.

One of us obviously interrupted her and asked if this friend was a schoolmate.

My grandmother smiles and says she had no idea who this girl was. She'd have lunch with this mystery girl in their school garden, but she'd never hear from her or see her otherwise. In fact, she doubted if she even belonged to their village. They never spoke to each other; they just sat under the shade of the school's huge banyan tree and shared their lunch with each other. My granny would then go back to her classroom, and this girl would wander off, out of the school grounds. Apparently, the mystery girl ate the same meal every day. She'd bring it packed and tied in a banana leaf. If my grandmother tried asking her questions about herself, she'd merely smile or nod. And so, she decided against asking her anything and instead focused on finding comfort in the silence they shared.

One Sunday morning, my grandmother and her extensive family prepared to visit the neighbouring village temple. As they anticipated a lengthy journey, the entire family arose at four in the morning, packed their lunches in steel boxes, and set off for the temple. To her surprise, my grandmother was in for quite an experience.

The temple they visited was vast, adorned with exquisite sculptures and paintings. Planning to stay until the following afternoon, they were directed to a temple room designated for visitors.

At around 6 in the evening, the sound of drums being played echoed in every corner of this temple. My grandmother, overcome by curiosity, followed the sound of these drums to the centre of this huge temple, and she marvelled at how beautiful the sight in front of her eyes was. Her eyes shone with pure adoration and surprise as she saw black-eyed beauties in their bright red saris and shining gold jewellery dancing to the beat of the drums and the musician's lyrics. They were all of different ages—some in their thirties, some a little older than that, and very few who were around my grandmother's age. As her eyes scanned some of those sixteen-year-olds, they finally landed on her mystery girl. She gaped in awe, her face full of amusement as she saw that girl's body effortlessly swaying and moving to the music. She could swear the girl saw her too; at least she caught a glimpse of her, but her face showed no sign.

My grandmother's thoughts were interrupted by the booming voice of the priest who came and stood next to her. Before she could open her mouth and voice the hundred questions in her head, the priest started speaking as though he understood her shock. A sandal-coloured cloth she identified as veshti was wrapped around the lower part of his body. He also wore some red-coloured kumkum on his forehead—a religiously important powder, my grandmother was told. He looked old, around forty or forty-five, my grandmother assumed. He had hair only in the back part of his head, and it was tied up into a small ponytail. The front part was bald. His neck was decked with a chain or two, again of religious significance.

"These women are called Devadasis," he started off in a voice laced with composure and wisdom. "They have decided to submit themselves to God and have dedicated their entire life to the divine supernatural deity. This was done before the attainment of puberty. They live in the temple; the temple provides them with all necessary living conditions in return for their service to God."

Overcome by shock as to how someone could spend all of eternity living between these 4 walls and with a hundred more questions, my grandmother finally asks, "And what if they want to leave?"

"They cannot, my child. At this point, they have married themselves off to God. No other relations are allowed. The temple is their home; they belong here," the priest replies in the calmest voice ever, as though he did not just talk of how someone marries a supernatural being.

My grandmother watches the dance for a while more before her mother comes and picks her up. She is tucked into bed, but she cannot sleep. Not after knowing that so many women just decide to live here forever. And once they make the choice, they don't have the option of reversing it.

These thoughts shroud her mind and keep her occupied for quite a while. It's almost midnight, and she still couldn't sleep. She looks around to make sure her family is fast asleep. Then she slowly removes her blanket and, slowly, she walks up to the door. She opens it as quietly as she can and sneaks out.

She aimlessly wanders around the huge area of the temple, for a while, she even sits by the lake and wets her legs. Then she suddenly finds herself following hushed whispers disturbing the calming silence of the night. She treads softly on her two feet, ensuring no one catches her lurking around. And when she finally finds the room from where the noise was coming, she tiptoes her way there and stands next to the door. Through the small opening, she sees the priest who talked to her earlier today. He seems to be talking to someone and looks angry. The rage plastered on his face terrorises my grandmother.

When she tried to see a little more clearly, she saw an old lady wearing a saffron-coloured cotton saree holding onto a girl. A girl with wheatish skin, a slender body, and black eyes filled with fear. Her mystery girl.

"What do you mean she's pregnant? It's not possible," the priest shouted. "I..I..I don't know, sir, but I'm sure she is. She-"

Before the older lady could finish explaining, a harsh slap landed on her cheek, leaving a red mark. The mystery girl shrieked in pain and fear. Now that my grandmother saw her in a saree, she realised she was a little younger than this girl. This girl looked around twenty or twenty-one, while my grandmother was just 16 at the time.

"I'm sorry, I -"

Not giving the little girl a chance to apologise either, the priest grabbed her by her hair and hit her head on the wall. He did it again and again until there was a pool of blood on the floor.

"Clean this filth up, I'll send someone to take her body away," he said, in a voice so composed it almost sounded like he did this every day.

When the older lady tried to rebuke, she was silenced with another harsh beating and a rant about how what happened was a sin and a mistake. Of how the girl was of no use to the temple anymore.

As my grandmother heard footsteps indicating the priest was going to leave, she ran as fast as she could, not worrying about her gasps echoing between the walls. She rushed into her family's room and shut her eyes, which were red and full of tears. She slept in her mother's cot, holding on to her tight and muffling sobs against her mother's saree.

From that day on, she ate lunch alone in her school playground, and not one day passed when she didn't think of this girl whose life she may not have known much about, but the bits she did know were tragic enough to scar her for life.

"But why would she choose such a terrible life?" my naive younger self had the audacity to ask.

"She didn't. If the priest could kill her, could he not lie to me as well? These Devadasis didn't choose their lives. Women from the lowest castes were forcibly taken into temples and compelled to lead these harsh existences. Lives where service to God took on an entirely new meaning, lives where they could easily be exploited," my grandmother replied, and I could swear I saw a tear escape her eye. It was the first time I had witnessed her cry.

"But why did the priest have to kill her for being with child?" one of my cousins pondered aloud.

My grandmother sighed, wiping away the stray tear. "Because it was his child."

6

WHAT THEY DON'T TELL YOU

As I listen to my teacher
Talking about the Nazis
As though it all happened overnight

I recall what I've heard and read elsewhere
I realise all that she doesn't tell us.
She doesn't tell us how

There were millions who were unfazed,
When there were people being gassed
People being raped, jailed and erased.

As she rambles on about the different years
I look around only to know
That none of my classmates realise
That fascism can rise to power

As we flip through our textbooks
That once upon a time
There was this German man
Who emerged as a saviour,
An angel in disguise they said

My teacher doesn't tell me
About how a mother spent all night
Outside the prison of her journalist son
For he wasn't one of those
Shameless yellow journalists
She doesn't tell me of how

The wisest chose to stay away from
Politics and its dirty games
As she states figures and numbers
She doesn't tell me
Of those who died of hunger

Of those who were threatened in their own land
Of those who faced unfathomable humiliation
Of those who were born in a certain race
Of those who were kicked and punched

All she tells me is that it happened far away
She shows me the symbols of the Nazis
Just for me to vomit it all out in my test paper

For it is but something that surely won't happen again
Something that will not emerge out of nowhere
And catch me by surprise

Of course, we'd be on our guard if

History ever decided to repeat itself

And most definitely it will not happen

In my own land, my own country

For we've been educated the right way

7

I Am

I am,
That pile of papers
On the clerk's table
Waiting to be signed
By that one minister
I am
That cup of tea

That you left at your table
Because you didn't drink it
Before it became cold
I am

That pending assignment
You postpone till
The teacher doesn't care anymore
I am

That rebel who was
Asked to quiet down
Whose hand was put down
Whose shouts were ignored
I am

A wrong to be righted
A bill to be passed
I am

That stifled sob
That suppressed voice
That banned article
That seditious thing
That bruised the ego
Of the minister who
Refused to hear me out
I am

But just another,
One of the many
Oppressed, Ignored and Discriminated
This country has seen.

8

DEATH: A MUSING

As I reached for the pen stand, I accidentally knocked over my half-drunk coffee mug. I silently cursed my luck and hurriedly grabbed a tissue from my desk drawer to clean it up.

The edges of my long-overdue draft were smeared brown with coffee. Well, it's not like they were going to end up on a publisher's table anyway. Writing was one of those dreams that kept me warm when reality left me cold—a dream I've pursued for as long as I can remember, knowing all the while that it's not something I'll be able to achieve. So, I work in a clerk's job, one as dry as dust. It was my last resort, given my educational background and the pressing need for financial assistance that arose when my family decided to sever ties with me.

My family—something I try my best to avoid thinking about. It opens old wounds. You see, I grew up in the remote village of Mauranigram, tucked away somewhere in the diverse country of India. Growing up, I was too progressive for a village as backward as mine. I didn't understand why my sister couldn't attend school with me. I didn't understand why my dad and I couldn't take my mother along to village council meetings. I didn't understand why my dad bristled with rage when I got involved in household chores. I didn't understand why it was okay to be friends with a drug-dealing bully of my religion but not with harassed, abused innocent boys who were separated from me by divisions of caste, creed, and religion—barriers that humans had erected by their own will, only to spew hate and abhorrence among themselves. I refused to keep my mouth shut and focus on the good, when all I could see were vengeful, prejudiced crimes happening around me. And so, I spoke up, I revolted. Naturally, I was asked to keep quiet.

I remember quite vividly that Thursday afternoon when I realised that my dad wasn't the gallant, courteous man I had looked up to. He caught me talking to Afrah, who hailed from a part of the village my father and his comrades considered as inferior. She was a Muslim, an outcast. I was forbidden even to look her in the eye. But there I was, in the middle of the street, tending to a wound on her smooth, chocolate-brown skin. I've learned to carry a basic first-aid kit in my bag always, as riots in this village are as common as snide bickering remarks slipping out of my grandmother's mouth.

Afrah had been assaulted by Ved, the son of our village head. He was heavily built, wearing a black t-shirt that clung to his sweaty muscles. His fair-toned skin glistened under the afternoon sunlight. All the boys were returning home from school when Afrah accidentally bumped into Ved and his group of snotty friends, whom I've learned to steer clear of over the years. Ved, aside from inheriting his father's physique, was just as superstitious. Thus, the fact that his skin had touched that of a Muslim girl had enraged him. He was fuming with anger and, in the heat of the moment, decided to hurt Afrah, leaving her crying in the middle of the street.

I knew that the wiser and more sensible thing to do was to walk away, just as the others did. But my conscience couldn't allow me to simply walk away and leave her crying.

When my dad saw me helping her, his blood obviously boiled. His cheeks were red, due to both the anger and the humiliation he felt from the disapproving looks of the passersby. He grabbed me by my collar and delivered a sharp, painful slap to my cheek. He then dragged me home and gave me an earful.

I remember every word of that conversation. In essence, it conveyed that if I interacted with people I wasn't supposed to, it would tarnish my family's honour and reputation. I couldn't care less about either, but my father claimed to have spent years building them up.

That was when I realised I couldn't spend one more second in my village. I had endured enough of being constrained by beliefs I would never comprehend or relate to. I also recognised that I was being delusional in thinking I could ever rid the village of its superstitions. Centuries of beliefs couldn't be changed by someone like me, so I thought it best to leave. Obviously, I needed more than just the few clothes I owned to start anew in a completely different place. So, for a few more years, I followed the path my father had already laid out for me. I got involved in my father's business and tried my best to remain silent about all the horrendous things happening around me. When I had saved a reasonable amount of money, I made the decision to leave. It might have seemed foolish to leave a village where I had everything and move to a foreign city to start a completely new life, but I felt I had no other choice. Every day I woke up in my father's house, I couldn't help but think about all the dreadful things he had done throughout his life.

On days like these, I find myself thinking how different life would have been if I had not caught that night train.

Once I've cleared the desk of the coffee stains, I remove my headphones and look around. It's almost midnight; my colleagues have left. I'm done with most of my work too. In fact, if it were only about the work, I would have left hours ago. But, you see, my colleagues have families to go back home to, and then there's me. Why go back when I know there's no one waiting for me to come? Since I decided to live this life, I've only had the sky coming to my rescue when it saw my reflection drowning in a stagnant pool of pain. Maybe it's my fault; maybe I found too much comfort in nature and all things not human, and hence ended up a loner. Although I'm not complaining, I would much rather go home to my plants and storybooks than party with a bunch of people faking smiles.

Am I happy, am I sad? It's a question I've failed to answer. You see, for a long time, I glorified sadness; I found it poetic. But over the years, I've come to know that no grand poetry is as real as reality. Darkness is real, but it isn't comforting. For as long as I can remember, writers have been romanticising sadness, describing it through metaphors so beautiful it camouflages the pain; they leave things unfinished, they chase things that get them nowhere. Writers make constellations out of scars, and readers devour fiction to escape reality. Sadness isn't the shade of autumn leaves; it's an ugly demon that prowls around, denying you joy.

And now is when I finally decide I'm done for the day; I shut my laptop. My eyes adjust to the loss of light. I rummage through my leather bag for my bike keys. It doesn't take too long to find them because all the bag has are a few mints, my diary, some pens, and my wallet.

I lock the office door and leave for my house. Another day of feeling as empty as the moonlit streets. Another day of contemplating the decision I made. Another day of missing my mom, cursing my dad, and pitying my sister. The weekend is here, which means I have two days to myself. Any normal person would be happy. But work helps me keep my mind off things that keep me up at night. I just know that the next two days I'll find myself thinking and overthinking all that I have done in the past twenty-five years of my life.

And so, I go home, completely aware of my useless existence.

I let out a lazy yawn, and after snoozing the alarm a couple of hundred times, I finally decide to wake up. It's almost one in the afternoon. I hear my phone ringing. That rarely ever happens, since the only people who ever call me are my boss and my landlord. Considering I don't have any pending drafts or deadlines to meet, and I paid my rent only yesterday, I wonder who it could be.

I reach for my phone at the end of the bedside table, still slightly drowsy from my sleep. It is an unknown number. Usually, I decline such calls, but for some reason, I decide to pick up the call. The speaker is silent for the longest time, and just when I'm about to cut the call, I hear a whimper, a cry of pain, of despair. I hear a voice I could never forget. The voice that sung me lullabies when innocent people would be slaughtered to death on the streets. The voice that comforted me while tending to the bruise my father gave me. The voice that begged me to stay when I was about to leave. My mother's voice.

"You're dad's dead," my mother finally says.

I try to feign indifference. I try to act like I'm not triggered by his death, like my heart doesn't ache because I couldn't bid him a proper goodbye.

"You should attend the funeral," she says when I don't say anything. "I cannot, and you know it," I reply in a heartbeat, without thinking.

"Despite all that happened, he's your father. Your own blood. You want to come; we both know it. Don't let pride cloud your sense of judgement."

I've wondered all too often how one deals with the death of someone they love more than life.

Do you just embrace it? Or do you mourn until you join that person somewhere on the other side? Does it just come and go? Or does it brutally ruin your existence?

Death finds its way into your body the minute you are born. And it sits there for days to come. It slowly starts eating you up, nibbling the smallest pieces at first. Suddenly, at one point, it feels like it's had enough; it succumbs to greed and mercilessly erases your very existence. Is it luckier for it to be sudden and unexpected? When it consumes you the minute you're aware of it lingering within you. When it decides to end you without giving you a chance to say your last goodbyes?

Or is it better for it to slowly finish you, while you die a million times a day from the pain? The pain growing within you and the pain you see in your loved one's eyes every day. Is it easier to go after seeing them being tormented, after seeing hope vanish a little more every day in their eyes?

Death doesn't just ruin you; it leaves behind its mark. It makes sure the people in your life suffer after you leave, so you don't reach peace, even in the afterlife. It is aware of the power it holds, and I've conjured up a hundred images of it smirking in its vain, revelling in its glory, and reminding us every day that it can cause us more pain than we can ever imagine. That it comes in any form. Be it the small puffs of smoke or fires that burn up cities. Be it the lack of water or an excessive amount of it. It has its ways.

Its pride naturally makes it ignorant. It doesn't listen to the prayer your mother says for you or see the tears your friend sheds every day for you. Its ears don't ring with the 'Please don't leave me!' or 'God help my child.' It is the graveyard in which you see a pyre daily on which the wishes and prayers of people are burnt. It punches you in the gut, pulls your heart out of your chest, and makes your throat bleed.

But death doesn't care. It's deaf to your cries, blind to your misery, and too dumb to give you an explanation. And that's not it, with death comes mourning, comes grief and sadness. The kind you've never experienced before, the kind that hurts you a tad bit more than death. For you see those you love suffer and break down in front of you, because of you.

Death is something I've thought about on more sleepless nights than one, something that had never directly come at me till this very moment. And although I might not have been the best son and he may not have been the most understanding parent, like my mother said - we're family.

Blood is, after all, thicker than water. "I'll come."

9

THINGS I'D LIKE TO BELIEVE

I'd like to believe that once people die, they find peace on the other side and bond with new people and watch over their loved ones from wherever they are.

I'd like to believe that humanity isn't completely lost and the glimmer of it I see in the eyes of my old watchman will not be lost when he's being humiliated and shouted at by the house owner.

I'd like to believe that God watches over us from up there and keeps giving us second, third, and a hundred more chances because he also thinks that one day all our hearts will swell with nothing but warmth and pure, selfless joy.

I'd like to believe that hate is too strong an emotion to be contained in any human body and is only an exaggerated form of dislike or disgust, and that it is not humanly possible to flinch at the mere sight of someone.

I'd like to believe that people develop friendships without the fear of being betrayed, get into relationships without the fear of being manipulated and used.

I'd like to believe that no human takes advantage of another human or traumatises and frightens them.

I'd like to believe that it is possible to confidently walk on the streets or book a cab even at midnight with no fear or apprehension.

I'd like to believe that Adam and Eve are somewhere around and are hoping for the world to not succumb to greed the way they did.

I'd like to believe that money isn't the most important thing and human relationships are valued more than any material possession will ever be.

I'd like to believe that kids don't carry guns around, men and women aren't violated cruelly, and murders and rape haven't become mundane headlines in the paper.

I'd like to believe that hearts break so that they can make space for more love, so that light seeps in through the cracks.

I think what I'm trying to say is that I firmly believe that there is still hope for things to be the way they should be, for us to make up for and repent for our sins. It's never too late to make amends, and there will always be a way to make things right. Let's give our future generation the world our parents intended for us to live in.

10

CARPE DIEM

Carpe diem exclamation
Used to urge someone to make the most of the present time and give little thought to the future.

I wake up to the sound of my father's alarm ringing, the noise loud enough to reach our neighbours. I check my own phone for the time, only to realise it's three in the morning. Why in heaven's name is the alarm ringing at this unearthly hour? My family is used to waking up early, but 3 in the morning is a bit excessive.

Then, I remember that we're all leaving for my grandmother's house today and staying there for the weekend. She's been feeling a little sick and lonely, and it's been a while since we visited her anyway. Only if we leave by at least 4, will we reach there in time for breakfast. I hear my mother barking orders, asking us to pack things at the last minute. It's the way things have always been in this household. I tug my blanket away and rub my eyes until I'm not as sleepy as I was two minutes ago. With all the effort I can muster, I get out of bed and go to brush my teeth. I also wake my brother up to save him from my mother's morning rage. We both quickly have our baths and get dressed.

My mother is packing things up and gathering the bags in a frenzy, my father's making sure we haven't missed any of our chargers or phones. My brother and I sit on the dining table chairs, not knowing what else to do. Our parents regard us with scorn for sitting idly while they're tense and pacing around the house a million times to check if they've missed anything.

We're finally carrying the bags to the elevator, and we get into the car. None of us speak; we're all annoyed and vexed because of waking up this early and all the confusion and chaos that ensued after. I badly want to ask my parents if I can connect my phone to the car and play music, but given their irked faces, I warn myself against it.

We're not always grumpy and fighting, but when we are, the air is so thick with tension you could probably cut it with a knife.

When we're halfway through, my dad suddenly breaks the silence and asks, "Where's my laptop bag? It has all the chargers and phones."

I have no idea why he randomly remembered to ask us this. But as sad as the fact stands, we can't go two days without our devices. So, we instantly open the back of the car to check for the bag.

When has luck ever been on our side?

We reverse and travel back all those hundred kilometres to retrieve the bag. My mom's expression tightens more, my dad tries his best to seem apologetic. My brother and I just sit there with our best poker faces, not knowing how to react.

We usually always check twice, for the fear that something might go wrong. No, for when something goes wrong. Let's be realistic. But this time, since we left early in the morning, we didn't. And so, we obviously had to forget something.

When we're nearly at our house, my brother whispers in my ear, "I bet if one of us had forgotten the bag, we'd be on the receiving end of taunts and scolding." The statement earned him a glare from both my parents. My dad rushes upstairs and gets the laptop bag. We resume the journey, or rather start it all over again. Now there's no way we'd reach before breakfast. So, we stop at one of the restaurants and quickly have a light meal.

And just like that, we're back in the car. The uncomfortable silence is killing me, but I can't do anything to change it. I very conveniently also forgot to bring my storybook for the trip this time, so all I had to do was stare out of the window and wait for this storm to pass. We're all engrossed in thoughts of our own, worry and anxiety loom over us. We think of what's to come, of how we'll overcome all the hurdles the future has for us. We also regret all that we've done, we think of how much better off we would've been if we had righted that one wrong thing.

Out of absolutely nowhere, my brother says, "You know why mountains are funny?" In a flash, I ask why, eager to break the silence.

"Because they are hill-areas. You know, because it sounds like hilarious?"

Him explaining the joke is the only funny part about it. But it stirs a laugh out of me anyway, because of his impeccable timing. And just like that, my parents also join the laughter, and we're done fighting the silent war.

Life's too short to pretend you don't adore the people around you. So quit fighting and revel in the beauty of survival and growth. We're all standing, sleeping, or sitting on precipices of our own. Where our past is an echo of what's over and our future is a shadow of what's to come. But for now, let's all together find joy in the present; it's not so hard. Worrying about what you've done is not going to change a thing. And about the future, well, the light's always going to be there at the end of the tunnel, no matter how dark or long. It's up to you to make it to the light. Memory is a frightening abyss; you never seem to do your best when it comes to memory.

There's always that one thing you could've done better. And the prediction of what you'll become is an illusion; it's an abstract thought coated with too many wishes and lies to ever be true.

Time watches over us all; it can end us anytime in the course of our diminishing existence. And I'd much rather spend it smiling instead of complaining.

Carpe diem!

11

REASONS GOD CREATED EMOTIONS

He knew that one day you'd come back home, your hands smeared in the chocolate your teacher gave you as a reward for winning the race, and you'd want to jump and dance and sing. You'd narrate to your parents repeatedly how you overtook that girl who almost won, how the taste of chocolate would forever linger on your lips, reminding you of victory so sweet. He knew you wouldn't be able to wipe that silly grin off your face when your friends praised you over and over again. He knew how your heart would flutter when you attended your first concert or read your favourite book, how your body would be filled with warmth when you knew you'd made your parents proud. And so, he created joy.

He also knew that one day you'd come back home after getting into a fight with your friend, that not every match he made-up there in heaven would work out. He knew that one day your boss would shout at you, that you might be on the receiving end of taunts and complaints. He understood that life might one day decide to show you how a little bit of struggling feels. He knew that on some evenings you may need to be reminded of the things you need to be grateful for, even if it's the hard way. He predicted those tears that threatened to spill from your eyes. He knew that one day your heart would break when someone you loved found their way next to him somewhere up there.

And so, he created *grief*.

He knew that you would flinch at the sight of that one street dog, its eyes bloodshot, carrying a murderous aura around. He knew that maybe one day the world might not be the safest place for everyone to walk around without a care in the world.

He knew what the sight of that one scary-looking ride would do to you. He understood the chills that would track their way down your spine after you watched a horror movie or read a scary book. He understood your impulsive thoughts and overthinking that would get the better of you, leading you to believe that every other thing is a threat. He saw it in the eyes of the mother who sent her daughter away to college and the father who handed over his son to the military. And so, he created fear.

He knew that one day you'd come back home tired and bored. When you feel like life has lost all of its meaning and your mere existence annoys you. You're suddenly extremely aware of the curves in your body, the acne on your face, and the pits under your eyes. All your failures make up a list in your head, and you read it over and over again. He knew that you'd suddenly be ready to swap your life with all these people you see through a tiny little screen. That you'd regret choices, be envious of others, and hope and wish for life to be different. You'd complain and bask in self-pity. You'll land yourself in a hellhole where you'll continually question yourself about what you're doing with life. And so, he created disgust.

He knew that one day you'd create a void in your chest almost as deep as the bags under your eyes. That you'd want to dump all the betrayal, the sorrow, and the suffering you've seen along with the bodies of those who caused it. You'd feel your skin tingle with something dangerous, something capable of causing more ruin than you can fathom. Something only you have the ability to control. He probably even saw you sitting there on your couch, stalking someone on social media, resisting the urge to throw your phone across the hall. He knew your eyes would turn blood-red from all the crying and regretting. He knew your hands would tremble with the urge for revenge. And so, he created rage.

He also knew that one day you'll find yourself at peace. You'll find yourself somewhere you never expected to be, doing something you never imagined yourself doing. You'll love every second of the life you would have managed to weave for yourself, and you'll surround yourself with people who feel like sunshine. He knew that this is where you always wanted to be; you'd just never admit it to yourself. You'd be amused because if someone told you this is where you'd be 10 years ago, you'd laugh. And so, he created surprise.

He just always knows. And I may not know as much as he does, but I've always found it right to follow the heart and listen to these emotions, for I'd rather live with consequences than regrets. Because that is life, messy, complicated, and occasionally beautiful.

12

SELFIE

I tug on my sweater a little extra tight as I stare at the misty landscape ahead of me. It's no Switzerland, but it is breathtakingly beautiful. The mountains stretch as far as my eyes can see, their tips covered in fog. two cows are walking around on fresh, wet grass. My brain thinks of all the poetic ways to describe this view. Tiny drops of rain fall slowly, clearing the mist, adding even more beauty to it all.

We are on holiday in this small hill station tucked in one of the corners of the state I was born in - Tamil Nadu. My mom and I spend moments gaping at the view while my father and brother buy tickets to get into one of the garden-parks.

We stand there, rubbing our hands to keep ourselves warm. I hear a faint noise behind me, someone shouting something, calling out for someone. I turn to look at a man in his early twenties shouting at my mother and me from across the road. He seems to be saying 'Selfie' repeatedly. Involuntarily, I rush to their side to help the old lady cross the road. She holds onto my hand, and her husband and the man follow behind.

'Selfie' is all he says again. My mother assumes he wants us to take a photo of them. So, we ask them once again if that's what they want, just to confirm. He shakes his head in denial and pulls out his phone, taking a picture of the 3 of us - my mom, him, and myself.

CLICK

He smiles and offers his thanks repeatedly. Later, in an attempt to explain himself, he says in broken English something that seemed to indicate, "I wanted to keep this memory, so I took a picture of us to look back on our trip; my grandmother wished for it."

It all happened so quickly; it took me a moment to wrap my head around it. When I finally found a grip and looked at my mother's face, I saw something that looked like fear and apprehension. I wondered why, but only for a split second. A stranger on the street had a photo of us, a photo of us with him. That thought should easily scare anyone.

I try to say something, but there's a lump in my throat. Fear has made a pit in my stomach too. I'm still partially in a haze; nothing like this has ever happened before. You see, my mother and I belong to that group of people who simply cannot say no. We feel guilty when we take a stand for ourselves or put ourselves first; it's almost as if we're offending someone else by doing so. It's not like we were given a choice here, but we could've moved away in quick denial. We could've walked away or raised our voices in refusal. But we didn't. We felt sorry for the old couple, and we succumbed to the humanity inside us. We forgot all of our presence of mind in that one small moment.

My father and brother approach us, and when we tell them what happened, my father brushes it aside as something menial and mundane, although he's slightly disturbed on the inside too. My brother, on the other hand, doesn't understand the repercussions of the situation, of how dangerous Photoshop and artificial intelligence have made this world. He's naive and unaware and doesn't understand why we're all so perturbed by one selfie. His innocence makes me smile; it fills my heart with hope.

My mother is anxious on our drive back to the hotel room; her fingers fumble, and her lips quiver. The latest news articles about more rape and murder cases only add fuel to the raging fire of worry burning in her heart. Her mind weaves a hundred different ways of how that picture could be misused, of how our lives could be jeopardised because of that one selfie.

Although I'm quite unsettled as well, I know worrying is going to do me no good. Our family driver hears of the same story, and in an attempt at consolation, says they were probably just villagers who wanted to show off the places they'd gone to and the kind of people they'd met there. How the difference in landscape and atmosphere between villages and this place fascinated them.

My mother scoffs at the ingenuity of the idea, of how it's too good to be true. But that truly got me wondering - what if he truly was a naive village boy who wanted to remember us with a photo? What if we're making too much of that situation? What if not all humans are as vile and untrustworthy as we make them out to be?

And just like that, the situation haunts all my "what ifs," putting me in deep thought.

TRUST. I've heard people talk about how difficult it is to gain but how easily it can be broken. It's like glass, they say. Fragile, to be handled with care. One wrong move and it's broken. In today's world where you need to look for humanity in every nook and corner, where everyone is supposedly selfish and guided by motives for their own good and success, even if it is at the expense of bringing others down, I can see why trust is as valuable as it is. People are taken advantage of, misused by the ones they've loved so dearly. Tragedies have now moved from novels to newspapers. Every day, my dad reads out something horrific and gruesome as a warning for us to stay safe.

We've all built these high walls around us, and the gates to our forts grow smaller and smaller after every betrayal experienced and every tear shed. Every time you talk to someone new, every time someone's overly nice to you, or every time you give your contact to someone you've just met, your radar goes up. There's always an ulterior motive; no one's selflessly nice because that's obviously not how the world works. This is what we've been told growing up, in school and at home.

And so, you find yourself overanalysing what you do, where you go, and what you wear. Am I being too friendly? Is my dress too short? Isn't this place too secluded to be visited at night?

I find myself hoping yet again. I find myself begging God to someday make this world so nice a place that we can all widen these small doors of ours. That we can all be capable of letting people inside our fort, with no fear and no apprehension. And when we do, we'll find a version of ourselves so outgoing and fun. A version you'll fall in love with, and you'll start sharing nightmares and your wildest dreams with random strangers knowing they won't hurt you.

We'll all give ourselves time to slowly let our walls break down. When all of us will together understand how important the word 'Trust' is to humans, and we'll value it so that we can make this world safe and sound for everyone once again.

So, we'll all look past our walls and see each other for the real person we are, and we'll hold each other's hands till the very end.

It'll take time, obviously, but Nelson Mandela once said, "People must learn to hate, and if they can learn to hate, they can be taught to love, for love comes more naturally to the human heart than its opposite."

And nothing could ever sum up what I feel more accurately because, as many long, boring speeches as we've heard, change starts from within you. So, while sitting on the car seat next to my mother, fervently praying to God that nothing untoward should happen with that picture, I vow to myself to become someone worthy of something as precious as your trust.

Someone who'll make it clear that in a world where trust doesn't come too easily to the human heart, if you decide to trust me, I will always wait for you to open up and be there always. I know how it feels because we're all the same. And I'll do the little bit I can to change that.

My trust has always been something easy to earn. I like to believe in people, given the silly optimist I am. But it's a bridge burnt very easily; it can quickly change from a blooming forest to one set on fire. It's happened before, and it'll happen again. But I'll take the risk because if it ends up in a situation where I'm taken for granted, at least I tried. And that's better than just sitting around, afraid, and insecure.

13

7 DEADLY SINS

Pride

You see me in the eyes of that vain man who declines your advice and goes all out to do it on his own. Will the glory not be shared if you help him? You hear of me when your grandmother tells you the part the mighty Raavan played in the popular Ramayana. I am also what you see in the eyes of the father burying his martyr son, wrapped in the tricolour. I am what you feel coursing through your veins when you achieve something huge and are at the receiving end of praise and fame. I am the one who controls the reins of the chariot of your life; I might lead you to your doom or just perform my duties and be off.

Greed

I am what whispered to you in your ears when you were a kid, to take that one last snack piece lying on the plate and pop it into your mouth. I am that coin you drop into the well, wishing for a fairy tale, but you always forget to wish for a happy ending too. You see me in the eyes of that man who didn't mind getting some dirt under his nails when he was climbing the ladder to success. I am also what motivated you to work more and strive harder for what you long to do. But, mind you, I don't like becoming an obsession, for then I'll offer you the shovel, and we'll both dig your grave together.

Lust

I am what leads the wisest, the most gifted toward their own rack and ruin. I am the undesirable side effect of love. I trigger thoughts that are uncalled for. I am what waged the biggest wars in history. It is because of me that your mother asked you to sit properly when you were young, it is because of me that you wrap your jacket a little extra tight around your body when you're walking at night. I am that high that loses its essence after the zesty moments pass. I am the cause of that headline that makes you shudder. So, forgive me for making this world an unsafe place; I am but just another sin.

Envy

I am what made you stare at yourself in the mirror, wishing more than anything that you were more like that girl in school. Fit, pretty, and popular. Or I am what bruised your male ego when a new popular guy came into class. I start infiltrating your actions as petty comments you make, pretending you don't care. And then slowly, I become an obsession; you do everything in your control and more to replicate that person's actions. You become consumed, and somewhere in between wearing fancy clothes and choosing popularity over comfort, you lose yourself. You're so far gone that you can't find yourself anymore. Your identity is merely a ruin, filled with the things that made you, YOU. And now you're just another one of the many trying to be that epitome of sought-after perfection.

Gluttony

I am what started off as that one drink your college mate offered, just for the thrill of it, they said. And now you find yourself driving in the middle of the night under the influence, pretending it's just having fun with life and not an unsafe addiction that will ruin you. I am what your parents warn you about when you're a kid. I am what starts off as one bottle and ends up as a hospital case. It is because of me that you walk on wobbly legs with bloodshot eyes, having given up on life. So, you gulp in shot after shot until it consumes you and kills you from the inside. Till everyone around you begs you to stop, but you've come too far anyway.

Wrath

The rage that radiates through your body, making you want to do the worst things, that is me. When you lose sight of reality, when you no longer think rationally, in fact, you forget to think at all. Revenge, vehemence, and hate come to you as easily as love once did. The sight of someone or something fills you with so much repugnance that all you want to do is watch them burn and turn into ashes. Your fingernails look like the sharpest of knives, forged in the furnaces of anger. Rage is not what poets romanticise and put into pretty words; it is unimaginable madness. It is when you'd wish to dump the bodies of those who wronged you in the same graveyard you dumped your love, joy, and hope in.

Sloth

I am what leads you into practicing what they call procrastination, a little minx that one is. What coaxes you into watching that one more episode, but somehow you find yourself glued to your couch all day. And when the show's finally over, realisation hits. Another day gone to waste, one more time when you succumbed to your own need for pleasure. I am how you somehow find yourself cuddled up in bed doing something that's definitely not your pending assignments or deadlines. I am the drowsy feeling you try to shake off when you're working at midnight, but I win too easily because you're asleep in no time.

No one is free of them all, but I guess controlling them is the trick. I wouldn't know, for I am a slave to these sins as well. And atoning for them is what I strive to do, or rather what my excuse is when I succumb to each of them.

14

GUNS IN SCHOOL

Amara aimlessly scrolls through her Instagram as her math teacher continues to ramble on about trigonometry. She couldn't care any less for school and studies; she has dreams of her own, not quite related to academics. But you need a degree for everything, so here she was in another one of those American boarding schools full of children with different hopes and aspirations. Some children were sent here because their parents wanted to get rid of them, some because their parents no longer live, and the rest who hoped to see their parents in a week when vacation starts.

Amara's mother died as soon as she was born, post-partum haemorrhage, they said. But she loved her dad unconditionally, for he had been to her the best single parent one could ask for. He believed in her and her dreams, and she loved him for that. She couldn't wait to see him next week, devour ice creams and pizza, go running with him at daybreak despite hating his annoying habit of waking up early, and most importantly, she couldn't wait for all the conversations they'd have, to tell him the million different things she couldn't convey over a text or a call.

As she heard the bell ring for the next class, she opened her timetable just to let out a silent groan. If there was one thing she hated a tad bit more than math, it was physics. She quickly asked permission for a bathroom break and slipped out of class.

She shut herself in one of the bathroom cubicles and started to look through her phone again. Scrolling through the perfect lives of Instagram models and celebrities may not have been the most entertaining thing to do, but it was what she preferred to physics class. And, well, she didn't have too many friends.

She was the introverted kind; she was her own best friend and worst enemy. She had a hundred voices inside her head to keep her company. She had woven her own imaginary world and characters for herself. Amara, to this date, had never been able to understand how people get bored when they're on their own. It had always been one of her favourite things to do. Music, food, and her dad were all she had ever needed.

She looked at her watch to realise she had been here for almost 20 minutes. She bolted open the door and took a minute to glance at herself in the mirror. She had her cardigan on to cover her thick arms, she was wearing a t-shirt that hung loose over her curves, and her skin was tanned from the hot Florida sun. Her skinny jeans clung tight to her skin. Her emerald-green eyes reminded her of her mother, whom she had only seen in pictures and heard about from her father.

She stopped staring at herself when she heard footsteps approaching. She watched as Emma entered, in her black shiny boots that screamed 'rich family's spoiled daughter.' Her tight little skirt and crop top highlighted her fit waist and skinny thighs, her flawless skin and perfectly applied makeup made every head turn. But if that was all, Amara wouldn't be so triggered by her presence. They had history, the kind that's tainted, the kind you think about when you can't sleep, and the kind you'd give an arm and a leg to erase from your memory. And she wasn't one to easily forgive; she held grudges like mothers held their infants.

Emma's popular girl persona is no secret to the school, but the bullying that comes attached with it may not be so obvious. It's always been reserved for those who are either too skinny or too fat, too dark or too fair, who eat too much or eat nothing at all, who talk too much or who prefer not to talk at all. To nobody's surprise, Amara's been on the receiving end of the bullying, the perfect target she was. She was meek, introverted, and apparently, fat. The menacing sneer Amara got from Emma as soon as she entered the washroom was enough for her to put her guard up, raise the walls of her fort of insecurities, and visibly flinch. She quickly washed her hands and was about to be on her way out when she heard a loud bang. The kind that'd make your ears ring for a while, the kind that'd make you jump on your feet and make you want to run for your life. She heard the unmistakable sound of a gunshot.

She felt someone grab her arm and rush her into one of the washroom cubicles. And so, she found herself stuck inside with her bully when tortured minds were handling guns outside on the grounds of her school.

When she finally manages to gather her thoughts, she looks into Emma's eyes. She sees something she's never seen in those bold brown eyes before; she sees fear and apprehension. She realises that Emma is scared for her life. Emma hasn't let go of the grip she had on Amara's hand. Amara feels it trembling, she sees Emma being vulnerable. It's heartbreaking, seeing those confident eyes laden with panic and trepidation. As much as she disliked Emma, for better or worse, they're stuck with each other, and so she decides to keep the past in the past. She hugs Emma, offering all the warmth and comfort she has to offer in that one embrace. She soothes her, calming her down and offering words of comfort.

She tells her it'll be alright, even though she believes otherwise.

She tells her they'll get out alive, even though she's internally preparing for the worst. She tells her no one will find them, even though her spine tingles with the same fear.

Emma finally manages to pull herself together; she wipes the tears from her eyes, smearing the perfectly put mascara in the process. She takes deep breaths and finally opens her mouth.

"For what it's worth, I'm sorry. I might not live to see another day, and I need to get things off my chest, things too much for me to take with me to the grave," she starts off, her voice shaking with fear.

"As silly as this sounds, I didn't mean to hurt you or anyone else I've bullied," she continues. "Emma, you don't need to," Amara hears herself saying.

Emma shakes her head and says, "Just let me. I grew up in an orphanage; I don't know who my parents are or what they do. I've never bothered to question it either. Not like I had a choice either. My orphanage was nothing like the one you'd read about in those beautiful books. You'd be given stale bread and cold porridge every day. You'd be beaten with a belt, and the warden would shoot you glares if you didn't finish your food or get to bed on time. My childhood wasn't all roses and sunflowers."

She stops for a moment, breathing heavily before she continues to pour out things she's never said aloud.

"And then finally, when I was around twelve, this rich couple who hadn't been able to have kids decided to adopt me. Just when I felt like things were getting better for me, God decided to remind me of my cursed fate yet again. When they drove home from the orphanage with me in the back seat, their car ran off a bridge. I was pushed out of the car by my to be mother who was sitting next to me. And I inherited their house, their money, and I've been living with the guilt ever since," she manages between sobs. "Bullying is a coping mechanism, as messed up as that logic sounds. It gives me power that kind of overshadows the guilt."

Emma had never said it all out loud until that moment. And the heaviness of the air when it's all out is suffocating. But it also feels like the chokehold it had on Emma all these years is gone. She feels free with all of it off her chest.

Amara is quiet; she's in a trance. She's taking it all in. Before she can reply, she hears another bang, this time from somewhere too close by.

Emma pulls her up, and they both stand on the closed toilet seat to avoid the risk of their shoes being seen through the opening below. They both hold their breaths, making sure not to make a single sound. A meek whisper, a helpless cry could cost them their lives. They hear footsteps walking around for a minute or two; in fact, one of the shooters even opened one of the cubicles. The girls silently thank God for their luck. When they finally hear them leave, they decide to stay there for at least another hour before leaving.

And there it is again, the elephant in the room, the issue to be addressed. The chances of their survival increase by a few more figures, which means Emma might have to spend the rest of her life knowing Amara knows of her past.

Amara cannot find the right words to express how deeply sympathetic she is toward Emma, but unsaid sentences somehow reach the other person in that small cubicle.

An hour goes by, and the girls spend it in comfortable silence. They both enjoy each other's company; they've finally found a friend in each other. If only they had realised that earlier.

They leave the bathroom on tiptoes, look around from the bathroom door. The smell of fresh blood fills the air, but there's no sign of the shooters or the sound of gunshots anymore.

Assuming they've left, the girls walk through the corridors to their classroom to collect their bags. As they pass each class, they see boys and girls shot in different places, lying around. They see their teachers staring with an idle look in their eyes and blood smeared on their clothes.

They are somewhere in between feeling grateful they survived and guilty that they did when so many didn't.

As they pick up their bags and make their way to the exit door, Emma says, "So I'm forgiven?"

"Of course, you are; it's all water under the bridge," Amara smiles. She's never been one to forgive, but Emma had a reason, a valid one.

"Are you okay?" Emma asks. "Right as rain!" Amara smiles back.

They walk out holding hands and giggling, just to be interrupted once again by that fatal sound. Amara feels the hand beneath hers losing life, going cold. She tries to hold Emma as she falls to the ground because of the bullet in her back. Although in a daze, Amara hears one of the men with the gun asking another to shoot Amara too. But the other complains and says he's out of bullets. And so, they leave the school grounds.

Amara cries until her eyes have no more tears to shed. She shouts until her throat bleeds. Her hands tremble as they are covered in the blood of the friend she made.

And so, another human dies. Another politician goes to sleep on his luxurious bed. Another mother gives birth. Another gun is sold. Another child is asked to handle a gun. And the world keeps spinning.

EPIPHANY

The birds find their way
    Back into their nests
Fathers and mothers
Children and teens
Find their way back home
The petals of the flowers close
And the owner of
The nearby small shop
Prepares to bring the shutter down
The sound of the waves
Hitting the rocks
Soothe some, annoy the rest
The city is full of
Houses so small and
Skyscrapers so big
Some lit till late in the night
In contrast to the others
With their drapes down low
And the sun decides to set
On our wins and losses
And so, the day went by
Beautifully spent for some

And utterly cruel for the rest

But as I pass by

The city looks to me like

The start of an epiphany.

16

I WONDER

I've wondered all too often if there is a world inside those books I read, if the characters I fall in love with as I flip each page see me too. If they can hear my thoughts and look into my eyes. If they wonder how I'll abandon them, leave them when I finish the book and close it. Well, do they know how much I think of them once I'm done with the book? Do they know I ask myself what they'd think when I make a few decisions? That they've made their way into all aspects of my life?

Because that is the effect a book has on me. Do they think when they're sat by themselves on my shelf, that they mean just as much to me as these other books do? For then they should know that I've devoured each line of the book they were in, and I'd do anything to meet them. But I'm real, and they're imaginary, but what if it is the other way around, I wonder.

Do my gentle fingertips flipping each page hurt them? Or do they make them wish they could hold on to my hand? But does that thought scare them? Holding on to someone who could easily rip their lives away, crumble it, and fling it into the bin? Well, I must let them know that I read each page of their book like my life depends on it. That reading about them makes a bad day better, a bitter coffee sweet, and turns my frown into a smile.

Do they see me smile when they say something funny? Do they hear me laugh at the sarcasm I imagine their voices dripping with? Does my gasp when they get hurt not tell them enough? Does the fact that they have no story that mentions my existence bother them? Or does it offer them relief? Do they prefer another reader over me?

They see me through the pages; I see them through the words written about them, yet our gaze never meets. Should it bother me as much as it does? Do they get mad that I read about them so many times, or does it fill them with relief and the feeling of being free? I've always imagined that when you open a book, you provide the characters in it with freedom.

Do I kill him every time I shut the book? Does my opening the book bring him back to life?

If not for my annoying curiosity, I would've left the last chapter unread, for then whatever we both have would never have to end.

I keep wondering, for that is all I have to do; that's what books do to me. It's a world where I can be anything, do anything, and go anywhere. And so, I can't help but wonder how there are people who go on with life, unaware of the joy books have the capability of filling them with.

Because we take for granted all too often the greatness of our minds and all that they can weave up. If I cannot convince you through poetry, let me use science to tell you that colours don't actually exist outside the human brain; the world is just a dull, endless void of black and white. It is our hallucination that creates colours to cope with it all. The fact that everything perceived isn't real, and we can do anything with the thoughts in our head, is amusing. Technically, English is just a random assortment of chaotic noises we've programmed ourselves to perceive as a language.

It's fascinating, don't you think? That an author weaves something up in his/her head, decides to put it into words, it gets printed, and finally lands up in your hands. You're given a free pass into their imagination, and that's all levels of crazy to me. I have, to date, never finished reading a book and considered it a waste of time. But it's not because they've all been good; I've had my share of books with plots that go round and round only to end up nowhere. It's still effort and thoughts put into words, and that in itself fills me with sweet satisfaction. There is probably a word for the smell of the pages of the book. But to me, they smell like nostalgia. Because I've heard somewhere that the Greek word for return is 'nostos,' and 'Algos' in Greek means suffering. Basically, nostalgia in Greek means suffering caused by an unappealing yearning to return. And that pretty much sums up what books mean to me. Because life without books to feed my imagination would definitely be full of suffering and a persistent need to return. I regard books the way Newton regarded gravity; when he discovered gravity, everything else suddenly made sense.

This is probably the most random chapter of them all, but I felt the need to offer my deepest, kindest appreciation to these books and their authors that have taught me things, comforted me, and helped me get through situations. So, this is an ode to books, to characters, and authors.

Thank you for engaging in mindless conversations with me in my head, even though you're unaware of my existence; it means a whole lot.

17

THE VIRUS

"Your dad and I have tested positive," my mother announced. "We just received the RT-PCR reports. Both of you need to stay in isolation for a few more days. Since it's Omicron, it shouldn't be severe."

She said it wouldn't be severe, but her fatigued voice, drooping eyes, and dry cough indicated otherwise. Dad had been ill as well, ever since he'd returned from the office trip. But how is he to blame? He was asked to go, and he did all possible things to procrastinate the trip, but no, he was compelled to go.

I closed the door, removed my mask—which for the past two days had been my regular apparel—and passed on the bitter news to my brother, who had just woken up. Both of us had been living in the bedroom for the past few days. Thankfully, inside the bedroom, we had a smaller room—the pooja room—which is why we managed to remain in isolation together (because we weren't ill) without murdering each other for two days. We would take turns attending online classes; he would attend one period in the pooja room, and then the next period I would have to.

We did enjoy ourselves the first day, eating and sleeping on the bed, enjoying the indolent, lethargic lifestyle. The next day was fine, but we kept hoping more and more that Mom and Dad would get better, that we wouldn't have to live in separate houses inside what was our joyous home.

So, after my brother and I found out that our parents were COVID positive, we obviously weren't too happy. But we promised each other that we would cooperate, we wouldn't fight or shout, causing more trouble for our poor parents. We consoled each other (which is very rare). I saw tears trickle down my brother's eyes; he had finally shed this manly, bold face he had been wearing.

I wore my mask since I had to go to the nearby room to bathe. On my way, I saw my mother leaning on the kitchen slab for support, making dosas for all of us. She could have ordered breakfast from outside, but she didn't want to put our health at more stake. Her hands were weak. Her temperature was high, she didn't say it was, but I knew, I did. Dad, on the other hand, was coughing—a dry cough, and yet there he was answering office calls. I silently thanked God for giving me the best parents in the world.

After bathing, I had my breakfast, and so did my brother. Today we didn't have it on the bed; we suddenly felt what we didn't for the past few days—a sense of wrong, a sense of guilt. We didn't want to do something Mom and Dad would've scolded us for.

Following this heavy morning, was a storm. One that was expected, the waves were high, the sky was thundering. And no, I don't mean a real storm. I mean one that brewed between my brother and me. Well, us not fighting for two days was a rare thing, great but rare.

It was his turn to sit in the pooja room, and the internet wasn't working there, so he began to shout and create a ruckus. And let me tell you, both my brother and I are quite short-tempered. Forgetting all the promises I made in the morning, the ones to myself, the ones to God, and especially the ones to my brother, I also began to shout. He came vand sat in the bedroom. I was fine with it; I sure was. After all, it was a free period for me. For a few minutes, he looked at me as though expecting something; he wanted me to leave the bedroom and go into the pooja room. But I couldn't; I also needed the internet.

And then we started throwing pillows at each other, hitting each other, pulling each other's hair, and whatnot!

Mom and dad, obviously stirred by the commotion, shouted as much as their parched throats would allow. They were worried, as they would be.

But my brother and I considered none of that a reason to halt our war. Amidst all this, his poor English teacher talked of unity.

We then somehow sorted it out, and I'd rather not take you through the brutal process. I then stood near the door, with my mask on, remembering to maintain a hurtful distance from my parents, and told them of how it was my brother's mistake. I narrated to them how he hit me and what he called me.

But I stopped short when I saw my mother's pleading eyes, though I could only see her partially through the door. She said no word because each time she tried to speak, her raspy throat would crack, scratching excruciatingly for every word that came out of her mouth.

I would nod, promising myself for the hundredth time that I would act more mature. My mom's dry lips would stretch into a thin smile. The thinner that smile got, the more the hope diminished. But we'll manage; we'll get through this—of course, we will.

I turned back, closing the door behind me, to look at a room too messy for any reader to fathom. Books strewn everywhere on the bed, the bedspread lay on the floor unfolded, my pens hither and thither, the pillows just as scattered. If mom saw that room, I doubt my brother would survive. I realise now that this prized 'Survival' I joke of is seriously at stake for millions today.

And then the day went by; lunch was awesome, for after all, it had the magical spice—Love. And today it was excessively sprinkled, despite difficulties. Classes got over; it was time for coffee. I put on my mask, went up to the door, and before opening it, I waited. I heard sounds from inside, shouts, and bickers.

"Oh no!" I sighed. Mom and dad were arguing. Asking for coffee now would be a wrong thing to do, right?

I didn't really open the door, or try to listen too hard, even though eavesdropping is my favourite thing to do. But I knew that it was a fight that was going to last. Mom ended the fight with, "Oh really? Then why don't you cook your own food?"

Until January 2022, God kept this virus away from us. We went on a tour, we went out of town many times, we went to Goa to look after my granny, yet the virus didn't barge into our house.

Maybe we weren't thankful enough to God, maybe we took, like humans always do, too much for granted.

If the virus hasn't knocked on your doors yet, then ensure it never does. Because newspapers and websites call it a virus that kills humans, but only the affected know it kills humanity as well. Remaining shut indoors with your family is, in itself, irking to the core; imagine being shut in different rooms, ill and fatigued. Fights are likely to occur, and hope is likely to vanish.

Remember where the first Omicron death occurred in India? In Rajasthan. That news sure did grab a place in the headlines for quite some time. People talked of the death for as long as it was the hot news, and then it was, like most other important things, forgotten.

This virus is probably to last for months more, putting our lives at the greatest stake, drastically affecting our lifestyle. But all I'd like to say, my dear reader, is that COVID isn't the full stop; it's the semicolon. When a writer uses a semicolon, he/she wishes to convey that the story is far from getting over; a lot is yet to come. Similarly in life, semicolons indicate hope, hope that nothing has come to an end, hope for each and every one of you who chose to fight. We all today are together standing on a thin line where we are given a choice, a crucial one: you either give up or you see how much you can take. Only if you have known melancholy, will you value joy and hope.

So yes, this too shall pass.

18

IT'S ALWAYS A CHOICE

There's a knock at my doorstep
A wounded soul, a tired human
Comes seeking for help
Begging me to give him
A place in my humble abode
And I do
For that's what I've always been taught to do
I see in this human's eyes
Gratitude and love

He tells me it was my choice
To help or to not
He wasn't dying
His face wasn't pale
And his mouth wasn't dry

He leaves, and I believe in him
Until I'm the one at his doorstep
I seek help, I seek shelter
He says he has no time

When I talk of the days he spent
Crying at my couch

He says it was always a choice,

I decided to take him in

Is he being cruel or practical?

Was I being kind or stupid?

I leave, having no other choice

Days pass by,

Sweaters are dug

Coolers are turned off

But tell me what I must do

When he stands at my doorstep

Yet again?

Telling me once more

That it is my choice

Do I take him in

Just for him to shun me out?

Or do I leave him

Cold and in rags

In the icy November air

I do what I've been taught

I take him in again

I repeat mistakes

I prepare for betrayal

19

DID YOU KNOW?

Do you know who Shah Jahan is? Yeah, so do I. The mad lover who grieved for all of eternity over the death of his beloved wife Mumtaaz Mahal. The man who built one of the 7 beautiful wonders of the world. He who built that huge building made of white marble, the one we fly all the way to the Indian capital to visit. Taj Mahal, the epitome of love, was built over two decades with around 20 thousand workers, elephants, horses, and a list of other things that proved this man's love for his wife who passed away giving birth to his fourteenth child. This is a tale passed down from my mother to mine, yours to you. But let me tell you something my mother didn't tell me. Years after his wife died, he got married. Not too uncommon in the days of the Mughals. But it gets worse; along with being the lover, he holds the title of the only Mughal emperor to have married his own daughter. This is the love we glorify; we popularise. Taj Mahal is no epitome of love; it's pride, guilt, and all things similar.

I just hope one day the world looks at Taj Mahal the way Mumtaaz would have wanted us to. A monument that reminds us of a woman so strong and resilient, the empress consort of the Mughal empire. The woman who married a man with 14 wives and yet, is the only one we remember till today. I hope we look beyond what ancient misogyny has passed on and put into our brains.

Do you know the Pythagoras theorem? Yeah, so do I. We've all heard of him, read of what he discovered. But did you know who his wife was? Theano, a philosopher. Pythagoras's favourite student. But we don't talk about that. We don't talk about how she helped him achieve what he did. How she stayed up late with him, worked out experiments with him. Because that isn't important; it's Pythagoras's theorem after all.

Do you know Pablo Picasso? Yeah, so do I. The great painter who created the most beautiful kind of art. His paintings held so much meaning, I've heard them say. But have you heard of his misogynistic opinions? Did you know how he physically and emotionally abused women for his own sweet benefit? Did you know what he told one of the women who fell into his malicious cobweb? He said to the poor lady that women were machines for suffering, that to him, there were only two kinds of women - doormats and goddesses. But we don't talk about that, of course, we don't. We only talk about his paintings, how remarkable they are.

Do you know Lord Brahma? Yeah, so do I. The creator of this world, according to Hindu mythology. Stories of his courage and bravery adorn scriptures and texts. They've been passed down to my family for generations before and generations to come. But no one talks about how he created the universe, of how his lust for his very own daughter, Saraswati, marked the first time a girl was taken advantage of against her will. This part of the legend may not be true, but for which part of mythology have we ever had proof? We've only believed what they taught us to believe. That's the way this world works. No questions asked; everyone lives in their own ignorant bubbles.

In a world where feminism has become a joke, where misogyny is by default administered into our minds, I hope the generations to come have a society that treats men and women equally. I hope they have religions that celebrate all achievements irrespective of whether achieved by a man or a woman.

When I speak of feminism, I mean equality. I see women taking advantage of what was wrought by the women of our past, after struggles difficult for me to even imagine, making a mockery of the rights we've finally won for ourselves after wars fought in public, struggles made in the privacy of our homes. I see women demanding things that are so far off the meaning of equality. I see us losing focus on what we need, going after mere wants. Silly, greedy choices and decisions we make that push us farther away from the concept of equality we've been dreaming of.

And so, the oppressed keep curling themselves into their blankets that offer them as little comfort as possible. And you know how we no longer talk of Pluto as a planet? Of how it's become something so many kids of this generation have no idea about. Similarly, one day we'll watch as equality fades into oblivion from an idea that was almost achieved, to a utopian reality we'll never have the joy of experiencing. Because we're used to our hopes skyrocketing only for them to get crushed on barren, dry land.

Revolt, fight, speak. Every part of my body shouts these words enough to make my ribs clatter. But what can just another person do? It's the only question that's stopping us from getting together and regaining clarity on where this must all lead us, on what the final aim is.

20

911

As you walk through the streets of Canada, covered in coats and mufflers on Christmas Eve, leaving marks of your shiny leather boots on the white snow, you'd see people buying gifts and trees. You'd see children playing in the snow. You'd see an old man walking his dog, looking for a nice bracelet to gift to his wife who is probably baking plum cakes back at home. You'd see couples walking hand in hand, or a family going out for dinner.

But if you ever get lost, as I quite often do, you might end up seeing this one building. I've never seen it, but I imagine it to be painted in a sober shade of brown or perhaps faded red. I wouldn't know. I also think it would be covered in snow, not cleaned too often. Since I haven't seen it, I also don't know how big or small it would be, but I assume it to be just enough to occupy around 5 or 10 people.

If you wipe the snow off those windows, made of glass, I assume, and you brush the snow off your gloves, you'd see this woman on one of those wooden chairs. She's handling the telephone in front of her, picking up calls every other minute. But during those precious one or two minutes she'd have, without the phone ringing, you'd find her staring at one object idly. You might think she'd have a hundred thoughts going through her head; she works at 911 after all. She hears of misery and illness every day: rape, abuse, theft, and fires - she's seen and heard of it all in her around 60 years of life.

But right now, she thinks of that one day, 30th May, was it? It was surely in 1979, she thinks to herself. She does the math in her head; it was her 25th birthday. She couldn't wait to get back home, receive the gifts, and spend all night talking to her friends. But she had to be done with her morning shift first. On that day, her mind was everywhere except her job. She thought of the places she'd visit, the wishes she'd receive, and the different things she'd want as gifts.

All that before she got that one call.

"911, what's your emergency?" she says in her best professional voice.

"All these messages get recorded, right?" the hoarse male voice on the other end asks.

"Yes, sir," she replies, lines of worry forming on her face, confusion clouding her judgement.

"Good, good. I can't reach my wife. She's been having a little bit of trouble with her pregnancy. I'm on flight 48, and it is going down," he replies, his voice sounding as composed as it can, but she hears the hint of regret, worry, and sadness in his voice.

"Your plane's going down, sir?" is all she can bring herself to ask; she's still taking time to process it all. This is not what she came prepared for when she wore her new dress and red heels in the morning. Not what she thought of when she blew the candles off her chocolate cake.

"Please just let me speak. I need to talk to my wife, and I don't have time. Just let me leave a message. Is that possible?" he asks, his voice now a mixture of frenzy and annoyance.

He's dying. He said something about his wife's suffering; she couldn't remember just what. His life is going to come to an end. He might survive, but how likely is that? How many times has one survived after leaving a last message? He's brave, she thinks to herself. She would have panicked if she were him, thought of all the things she wanted to do with her life. His voice sounded like he was in his early thirties; he isn't even done with half his life.

But instead of worrying, he decided to cherish that last moment. He decided to make the best use of what he has. She's snapped out of her thoughts by that man on the line.

"Miss, you there? Can I leave a message?" he asks. "Okay." That is all she can bring herself to say.

"Mariah, it'll be alright. My love for you will never die, even if I'm going to. Just take care of yourself. I love you. I can't reach mom and dad; tell them I love them too. Bye," he says before cutting the call.

WHAT JUST HAPPENED.

That's all the woman asks herself. A man is dying, a woman bearing his child will receive this news through a recorded call on 911. But doesn't this happen every day? Humans dying, their loved ones grieving. Fate weaving its cruel stories. It's no rarity. It's as common as some children dying of starvation while the rest have the largest variety of food to choose from.

She gathers herself, calls a higher authority to inform him of the plane going down. He responds with an assurance of taking necessary action. She glances at the wall clock. It's 12 in the afternoon; she can leave. Go back home to celebrate, to dance, and to sing.

And so, she does. She has no business feeling guilty for what happened to a random stranger. God, she doesn't even know his name. But she secretly hopes he survives; she hopes he goes back home to his wife and unborn child; she hopes he has the chance to bid his parents a proper goodbye. She hopes and hopes as she walks home.

She celebrates with a heavy chest; she dances with hands that should be praying for the families that will die in the plane crash. She sleeps on her bed, well aware of how grateful she must be for the luxuries she takes for granted. Her eyes finally close after hours of shifting uncomfortably, thinking of the grief those families must be experiencing.

She goes to her workplace the next morning, the events of the previous day still looming over her, haunting her like demons, following her like shadows.

She sees the higher authority she called to inform of the plane crash in the office. He has his usual monthly visiting rounds. This must be one of those, she thinks to herself.

He walks up to her, and she wishes him a good morning, even though her morning has been anything but good. He informs her of something that calms her nerves, that soothes the bugs crawling on her skin since that call.

"He survived."

Two words that mean nothing to a layman. But she knew who he was talking about. The man who had a family waiting at home. Mariah's husband. The caller.

She heaves out a sigh of relief. The sword hanging over her head vanished. Her body visibly relaxes. He's fine. He lived.

"The man on flight 48 who called you, he lived. I just thought you should know," the man says to her.

Suddenly, another alarming thought strikes her. The others?

As though he heard her thoughts, he said, "There were quite a few deaths. But some managed to survive."

Oh.

Death is inevitable; what was she thinking? That they would all survive. How naive. That some sort of miracle or blessing would prevent the plane from crashing. This isn't a fairy tale; this is not one of those books lying on her shelf nor one of those movies in her DVDs. Life and death, that's what they say.

And so, this woman proceeds to pick up another call after her two minutes of reminiscing and thinking.

And just like that, you find your way back; you're not lost anymore. You're on those pretty streets full of people wrapped up in fur coats, munching on burgers, and walking with headphones on.

Oblivious and ignorant.

Maybe not all of them. Maybe not you.

21

CHILDHOOD

Nothing will ever be the same again
which is to say,

you will never be the child you once were –

with melted chocolate and dirt smeared on your hands, your hair braided on both sides falling down your shoulders the taste of your mother's food melting in your mouth.

childhood is now a tapestry of memories and reminiscence you're so past it that you've come far enough when

your alone in the night with promises made, and

secrets hidden in the safety of the dark and burdens to be carried.

so that no shadow

reaches its hands into your school uniform.

oh the things you'll find in those pockets –

a note on a chit, pencil shavings, your innocence.

today, you regard yourself, cooking Maggi on the kitchen counter, writing poems so deep, your grief dissolves into words.

And some poems about hope. You're learning what it means to be another human in a world that can

barely hold your heart in its palm.

You're eating your maggi

with depressing music playing in the background. you are a villain in someone's story, but in yours, you're only a scapegoat chewing on protein bars and instant noodles.

but you still wish to believe in the good you're willing to learn how the world works

around nothing and everything at the same time.

You're body is a house of metaphors that made it off the page

you fall off the precipice,

a dark abyss swallows your weight.

Assignments to finish, deadlines to meet

you close your eyes and you think of the child you once were
Strawberries, crayons and squabbles full of bubbly laughter

You might never become the child you were

but you will also never not be the child you were It's the kind of logic

That makes sense in poetry.

22

Worst of Crimes

"Isha, are you ready?" her dad shouts, the blaring sound of his car horn reaching her window upstairs.

Sixteen-year-old Isha was indeed ready, dressed in her full-sleeved T-shirt and jeans, not too tight, not too loose, reaching down to her ankles. As she looked in the mirror, she asked herself, "Is there any other part of me I need to cover up? Parts that might entice men? That could lead people to talk about how I dug my own grave?"

She steps out of her house, sweating profusely under the July sun. Her light brown skin glistens under the scorching heat. She gets into the back seat of the car. Her father turns to assess her from top to bottom and finds her choice of clothing alright. With that settled, they start their journey to the district court. During the half-hour drive, they don't exchange a word. The radio plays, updating them with the latest news bulletins.

Upon reaching the court, her dad parks the car near a few other large vehicles, and they step out, only to be greeted by judgemental eyes, eyes that scrutinise their intentions and motives, eyes that accuse them of walking shamelessly in public despite all that has happened.

Everyone knew. Well, of course, they did; it was a front-page headline. They keep their eyes down and make their way to the entrance of the court. Isha takes a moment to survey the surroundings. The judge, a man in his sixties, sits atop his bench, casually handling his gavel as if it weren't the most powerful tool in the room. As if it couldn't condemn anyone to a lifetime of misery. As if the fate of her own family didn't depend on it. Next to him, on the bottom left, there's a court clerk typing things on his laptop, collecting pen drives, and reviewing the evidence through his wide-brimmed glasses. On the right, there's a witness box, where the truth can be spoken or twisted into something wicked, something that would shatter the hearts of those who know it isn't true.

Her eyes move to the place where the claimant and defence parties are seated. She takes in deep breaths; the situation is still too much for her to take in. But there he is, sitting on a swivel chair. She tries her best to look for guilt in those pitch-black eyes, only to find none. He looks different. He is no longer the boy she's known all her life. The boy who beat up the bullies who tried to hurt her, the boy she built forts with as a kid, the boy she sneaked out of the house with, the boy she played pranks on. She stares at her brother for a while longer before her father grabs her by the wrist and takes her there.

On the way, she steals a quick glance at the victim. Eyes laden with fear, she notes to herself. Her name is Sahana; she's seen her a couple of times before when she'd go with her dad to pick her brother up from college or to one of those parties where he'd get so drunk she'd have to escort him out.

Sahana is wearing an old, faded cardigan over a plain black T-shirt. It complements her slim physique. She's paired it with black jeans that cling to her skin. Isha feels the confidence draining out of this woman, her eyes tired of being constantly judged, her mouth dry after having to narrate the same story repeatedly because it didn't seem believable enough.

Her dad yanks her next to her brother as they wait for the lawyer to come. Her brother pins her with a pleading look in his eyes.

"I just want all of this to get over, Isha," he begs.

"And I want a brother who isn't a pervert. Newsflash—we don't always get what we want," she replies, trying to sound as bitter as she could. But the hurt that spreads across his face doesn't offer her the relief she thought it would.

Her dad whispers into her ear, "You better play your part well; I can't have my only son rotting in jail."

She ignores the chill passing through her spine. She ignores the bile rising in her throat. She ignores the tears threatening to spill from her eyes. She simply nods.

The lawyer finally arrives. Her eyes are as black as her brother's, her nose as sharp as Isha's own. Of course, their features are similar; it's their mother after all.

Her mother, Anjali Malik, a renowned lawyer who's been in the business long enough to know how it works, was defending her brother, Dhruv Malik, who was accused of sexually assaulting his college mate at a party when he was supposedly under the influence. The situation was truly too much to take in. Isha heard her mother spit out command after command to her brother about what he should do and how he must behave. Of how even the slightest change in body language could hinder them from winning this case.

And then she turns to her, their eyes locking. She finds an insignificant amount of emotion in her mother's otherwise bland eyes. Was it pity, maybe? Or compassion?

"Speak without stuttering and do not mess up," is all her mother says to her before getting back to digging into her files. It's the last day of the hearing.

The trial begins. The party that brought the case to court starts; Sahana's lawyer gets up. It's all happening so fast. Somewhere in the haze, she sees her mother standing up. Spitting out the so-called facts, pointing to the made-up evidence. She hears her mother shouting to cover up the potholes in the facts and statements. She feels her dad tense up next to her, anxious about what is to come. She sees Sahana from the corner of her eye, sitting still. Her eyes show no expression; it seems like she's already given up. Like she's lost her life.

She remembers that one day she went into that nearby pub illegally because she was underage, after her dad bribed the security. She saw Sahana dancing like it was her last day on earth. She heard her singing those lyrics at the top of her lungs like it was the only thing to do. Her hips swaying effortlessly, her mouth curving into a smile that could brighten up rooms. Her hands were all over the place. She looked like she was having so much fun. And then she looked for her brother, whom she was sent to pick up.

When she finally found him barely standing next to the bar stool, she was disgusted by the thin white lines next to his hand. She went over to him, shuffling between the crowds. She put his arm over her shoulder and led him out of the pub into their car.

She remembers all too well the way her father casually regarded his drugged son in the car but asked her to discard this dress of hers because it was too short. Double standards they called it, but she'd gotten used to it. It's what she's been trained to do, to adjust and to fit in.

Her mind then slowly drifts to that one night when her parents had a fight, loud enough to keep the neighbours awake. When her dad came home, drunk and sleepy. He had lost his job. He wouldn't tell the family why or how. He just expected them to understand. Only a few days ago, he had asked her mother to quit because families were gossiping about how she was one of the few women in the Malik household who went to work. But now she was the breadwinner. Her job was to pay the bills. It bruised her father's ego more than she thought it would have. But he had no choice.

And just like that, her mind drifts back to the court. To the judge saying something, to her dad motioning her to go. She was being called to the witness box by Sahana's lawyer. She stood on her two shaky feet, trembling as she walked to the front. She made her way into the box and held onto the railing so she wouldn't fall from dizziness.

"Miss Malik," the male voice addresses her. It was the lawyer defending Sahana. The lawyer she had been asked to lie to. He looked at her with hope in his eyes. He knew the truth; he knew her family was spitting one white lie after another. He hoped she wouldn't. How she wished she wouldn't have to let him down.

"Please go with Isha," she requested.

"Sure, Isha, you went to pick up your brother from Sahana's birthday party on Thursday, the 20th.

of June, am I right?" he asks. "Yes"

"Okay. Now this party was full of only college kids. Her parents were out of town. Just to confirm, you have no recollection of seeing her parents either."

"No."

"Right. When you went to pick Dhruv up, was there anyone else in the house?" "No, just him and Sahana."

"And did you see any signs of drugs or alcohol being consumed?"

Here goes the first lie. Do not stutter, she had been told. So, she lets that one lie spill from her rosy lips.

"No."

Isha had no idea that one lie would make her insides churn with guilt, but they did. She couldn't back down now; she had to keep going.

"Okay. Now you came here to pick your brother up. Where exactly did you find him?" Another lie; maybe it wouldn't hurt as much as the first one, Isha thought to herself. "In the living room, on the couch."

"Where was Sahana?" the lawyer asked, his voice persuading her to tell the truth. To get it off her chest.

What did he expect her to say? She found her brother on top of a girl, sexually abusing her. She decided to ignore her crying for help and just take her brother home. That image of Sahana, helpless and heartbreaking, of her eyes red with rage and shame both, of her face stained with the mascara that flowed down haunted Isha every single day.

"In the kitchen," she heard herself saying. "Who opened the door for you?"

"It was open; whoever left last didn't lock it shut."

That was one truth, at least. But what hurt was that her brother decided to take advantage of a girl in the open when anyone could enter.

"And you surely didn't see any signs of your brother assaulting Sahana?"

"No" One word made her body burst with guilt and shame. She didn't even dare to look into Sahana's eyes. The sorrow in them would make her spit the truth out instantly. But right now, acid has singed her throat.

"No bruises or marks? Are you a hundred percent sure?" his voice pleaded. "Yes."

A few more proceedings took place, none in favour of the victim. There were no cameras, and no one except Isha saw it happening.

You see, someone's always hurt at the end of any situation. You cannot drop a stone into the water without causing ripples; everything you do will affect someone or something else. It's the way our world works.

The case was closed. The court was adjourned. Her father drove the family back home.

But that didn't brush away the feeling of disgust inside her. The feeling of letting Suhana down The feeling of getting scared when her brother sat next to her in the car She didn't show it on her face, but it scared her to death.

She's heard people describe situations as ironic. In fact, she's found fascination in things like parody. Every time she'd see people offering flowers to the dead, she'd think of how ironic that one thing was. Of how we offer something that will ultimately die to someone who is dying. But what happened today was more than just another irony.

It's something that will haunt her forever—her biggest regret. She felt like puking out of sheer disgust as she heard her parents heave sighs of relief at getting their son back. She loved her brother more than anything in the world; she truly did. But right now, the voice in her head screaming that he deserves to rot in jail couldn't be silenced.

She was sad.

Sad that this happened.

Sad that she played a part in this.

Sad that her mother was paid to antagonise a victim, to celebrate, and to protect a criminal.

Sad that it is so easy to twist reality and convert it into fables of our own.

23

MY PURPOSE

I'll walk you through the streets of this small town
Barren lands, empty wells, fields dry and stomachs starving

It's a few miles away from the city I live in
And as I board my shiny yellow school bus I think of this old town
Of Ayesha, that girl who lives in that thatched hut
When her mother is out cleaning other people's houses
She dances and sings between closed doors
Like no one's watching, like a dream

Her hips sway effortlessly to the sound of her own sweet voice
But she's no star, she's to grow to do what her mother does
I think of Ayan, the washerman's son

He sits cross legged, learning to stitch shoes
When all he wants to do instead, is learn
To read and to write on those bright black slates
But he's just a village boy, why educate him?
Literacy is only for the elite and the well to do after all
I think of that sixty-year-old lady,
Who made her living through pottery,
She made the most beautiful looking mud pots

I think of the day she had fits and had to be rushed to a hospital

She would've survived if you turned up early, they said

Well, that hospital was two hours away, what'd you expect?

For them to fly,

But their wings are cut off even before they're born

So, they couldn't even dream of walking without

Carrying a load of worries on their shoulders

But why must I care, why must I think of them?

I'll serve my life's purpose and be off, fending for myself.

For life goes on for me in the city, for them in the ruins

They're aware of how those who live in primitive huts

Mustn't dream of lives in skyscrapers

24

HOW LONG?

"How long?" her dad shouts from the hallway. "We're getting late, Aditi. It takes an hour to get to the airport anyway, and with the Delhi traffic, God knows when we'll reach."

"Dad, no person in their right mind goes to the airport 4 hours before boarding time. You need to calm down; I'll be down in a minute," Aditi shouts back.

Her mom's sitting in the kitchen, packing the last of the pickle bottles to take all the way to Los Angeles. They're going to visit their son, Aarav, who goes to college there. It's the first time the rest of the family is going abroad. They can't wait.

And so, Aditi carries her huge suitcase downstairs and joins her mother as she packs almost the whole house to take to Aarav. Pickles, jam, and homemade snacks, all wrapped in aluminium foil and stuffed in Tupperware boxes, are packed into one big bag.

The cab had arrived at their doorstep, and they bid goodbye to their Gurgaon apartment for a month. It had been almost a year since they'd seen Aarav. Of course, there were video calls made as often as possible, despite the time difference making it a nuisance. They'd talk to each other, while on one end Aarav would be brushing his teeth; on the other, his father would be yawning time and again. But the family couldn't wait to reunite with the elder son. Aditi always felt he was pampered and loved a little extra, but which sibling doesn't feel that way? There's always that healthy feud with fighting for the TV remote or pillow fights that start with the silliest argument about whether Anime or Bollywood was the better source of entertainment.

But her heart also swelled up at the thought of meeting her brother, telling him about all the fun things happening at school, and sharing the new gossip in the neighbourhood.

They made their way into the airport, although they stopped for quite a while at the entrance, making the entire line wait. You see, her mother made the mistake of putting the purse with all the Aadhar cards in the bag with the pickle jars, so it took a bit of digging to find those.

But they finally got their boarding passes and went to the waiting area. After 30 whole minutes of convincing her father to get her a copy of the new Jeffrey Archer book from the bookstore at the airport, Aditi settled herself on one of the chairs, put on her headphones, and lost herself in the book in her hand. She kept reading for as long as she could, blissfully oblivious to what was happening around. Aditi was a girl of many dreams; she'd woven herself a beautiful future full of bright and beautiful colours, and she'd work to achieve that for herself.

Finally, her father pulled the book out of her hands and ushered her towards the long line waiting to board the flight. The scowl on her face because of the parting from her book made her father laugh, which only annoyed her more.

They sat on the flight, fastened their seatbelts, and got comfortable. Aditi's mother rested her head on the seat and smiled to herself. How kind life had been to her family, and she was grateful for it every single day. Her son had done well and secured himself a nice college seat abroad, her daughter studied well enough and would fend for herself, and both her kids were, most importantly, humble enough to acknowledge their parents for everything they'd done, unlike the snobbish fools she sees walking around the streets. No health issues, nothing unprecedented or bad. Life's good.

One glance at her face, and Aditi's father knew she was saying her daily thankfulness prayer, and so he did the same. Although they never admitted it to their children's face too many times, they were proud of what they'd brought them up to be and could only hope they stayed the same.

Aditi, on the other hand, had music blasting through her headphones and couldn't think of anything else till the plane landed.

They got out, went to the baggage pick up area, and collected their 8 bags. Aditi scanned the crowd for a whole 9 minutes before she finally found her brother waiting for them among the many people. He looked just as happy to see them as they were to see him.

Jokes and laughs were shared for a few minutes, and then Aarav collected the luggage and carried it to his car. They all sat in, Aditi in the front along with Aarav, who was driving, and the parents in the back.

"Wear your seatbelt, Aditi," her dad shouted.

"Will do, Dad. It's not going to make any big difference, but sure," she replied, half-heartedly. Her dad, on the other hand, always wore his seatbelt, no matter where he sat, front or back.

"There's no way in hell you got a pet snail!" Aditi asked Aarav, shocked at her brother's choice in pet animals.

"Don't talk bad of him like that when he's around; it hurts his feelings," Aarav replied with a perfect poker face. Aditi couldn't even tell if he was joking.

"What on earth do you feed a snail?" she asked, still in shock. "Human eyeballs."

Aditi didn't even bother replying to her brother's absurd answer. "Anyway, I was thinking-" Aditi started off.

"Oh, does it hurt?"

"Very funny," Aditi snorted.

They continued to talk about school and college, friends and enemies, and a truckload of other things.

"You conniving brat!" Aarav shouted when Aditi pinched him. "And you accuse me of eating a dictionary for breakfast!"

"No, I'm pretty sure you eat people's souls for breakfast." Their parents smiled to themselves, enjoying the silly banter.

The chaotic chit-chat continued. Aarav's parents updated him with the latest gossip back home, about the neighbours' daughter looking for a hand in marriage, where they not-so-subtly hinted at Aarav's marriage as well, and a bunch of other things. Aarav told them about the friends he made, his teachers, and life in general in a foreign country. His parents were glad he was having fun. Aditi asked him about the concert he'd gone to last week and the different things she'd heard about Los Angeles. Both talked about the long nights they'd spend fighting about the silliest things under the sun. They confessed to their parents about sneaking out of the house a day or two to get into a party and about a hundred other things they had to catch up on.

Loud laughs and lots of juicy gossip filled the car. Suddenly, out of nowhere, they heard a loud thud.

The car had been hit on the back by a rather huge vehicle. And the force pushed it straight ahead to hit another car on the back. The parents hardly suffered any damage since they were in the back. Aarav managed to maintain his posture and stay where he was, mainly because his seatbelt helped. Aditi, on the other hand, banged her head on the front part of the car, and blood oozed out of her head.

Of course, she hadn't worn her seatbelt. Her dad silently cursed, vowing to give her a piece of his mind once she regained consciousness. If she regained consciousness. But he wouldn't say that out loud, not even to himself. He heard Aarav calling for an ambulance, in a tone full of worry and panic. He heard his wife whispering comforting words, saying it'll be okay, more to herself than to everyone else. He then heard sirens, after what seemed like an eternity. Sirens, a sound he usually detested, a sound that reminded him of the night his mother died in an ambulance. But he brushed those thoughts away; that wasn't important now. Right now, he needed to save his daughter.

A stretcher was pulled out of the ambulance. Aarav and one of the hospital nurses helped carry Aditi to the ambulance, each putting one of her hands around their shoulders.

Aditi's mother held her hand, whispering the broken bits of comfort she had to offer. Aarav tried his best not to cry; lines of worry formed on his face, covered in sweat. Aditi's father prayed to all the gods, hoping against hope that his daughter survived this mess.

One reckless driver impatiently driving on the streets.

One person who refused to wear the seatbelt because of mere ignorance.

That's all it takes to weave a tragedy. But when will we ever learn? No stories, no lessons will ever make us reform our ways.

Finally, they reached the hospital, and blood trickled out of Aditi's left ear, evoking panic from her family. She was led up to the ICU, and her family wasn't allowed inside. They waited for around 20 minutes before the doctor came out. His face said enough, more than words could ever say.

The doctor started off in a voice full of empathy. "She is suffering from something called Traumatic Brain injury. It is commonly a result of car accidents. She is conscious for now, but the chances she'll survive are less." A stake in the heart would've hurt the family less.

The doctor looked like he was about to say something, but before he could, Aditi's father asked him, with a face that was too tired to show any emotion, in an empty voice -

He asked the doctor, "How long?"

25

Unsent Letters

Dear fear,

I get why you're a part of the emotion gang, I do. And I've seen you try your best to hinder and influence my decision-making. I plan on stumbling down the lane of experimenting, maybe even take confidence with me. And I know you'll be there, following us down every road at every step. You always do that.

I understand that it's something you need to do, something inevitable. After all, it's your job; it is why you exist. And it is solely because of you that I have lost countless opportunities to have fun and to do things I've regretted declining. The time I refused to put my name on the list for class leaders because I feared my friends would think less of me. The time I refused to step on the dance floor because I feared I'd make a fool of myself. The time I refused to read out my poetry to a gathering because I feared they'd think it was stupid. And the list goes on.

But I've made my decision, and it is important for you to know it as well. I want you to know that you can hitch a ride with me and the rest of the crew. You can get into your silly squabbles with joy, trying to subdue her. You can fight creativity to death. You can bond with my angst and nervousness.

But under no circumstances will I let you guide me. You will not tell us what to do or where to go. You will most definitely not manipulate us into going the opposite way; you will not be getting anywhere near the map of my life. And you most definitely will never be given control of the steering.

You can speak, but never decide.

Your presence is tolerated, not appreciated.

Your existence may not be the best thing in the world, but we've learned to keep you at bay.

Love,

Someone who's finally learned to conquer you.

Dear strangers,

Today was Friendship Day. As I stared at my wrist, full of colourful bands, I had an instant urge to thank some of you. I am obviously more than grateful for the friends and family God put in my life; they are the biggest rays of sunshine. But this is an ode to those of you who decided to be there for me in the heat of the moment, even when you had no obligation to.

An ode to the girl in the washroom who helped me wash the stain off my birthday dress.

An ode to the senior head girl who helped me get over the jittery nerves before a stage performance.

An ode to the random eighth-grader who sat next to me during lunch when both our classmates were absent.

An ode to that person on the street who helped me get up when I fell off my cycle and cleaned the wound for me.

An ode to the woman who saved me from a barking street dog during the evening.

An ode to another random schoolmate who decided to offer me 50 rupees when I very diligently forgot my canteen money at home.

An ode to the classmate who gave me a paracetamol when I wasn't feeling too well.

An ode to the random guy who came up with an excuse so that I don't get scolded for bunking class.

An ode to that little girl who ran up to me and offered me a chocolate for no reason I can think of.

An ode to the person who agreed to become my partner in a school activity when my best friend was absent.

And lastly, an ode to you, dear reader, because you decided to pick this book up. The fact that I get something as precious as your time and attention for my thoughts and musings will always mean a whole lot to me.

I might not remember your names and birthdays. In fact, I may not even be able to recognise some of you by face. But I hope you know I'm glad you decided to help me when ignoring was an option. If not for all of you, my day could've taken a turn for the worse.

Love,

Someone who's grateful you exist

Dear kindness,

I saw you in the eyes of that girl who helped another boy from hurting himself and lost her chance to win that running race. I saw you in the smile of a stranger on the street. I saw you in my parents' eyes when they offered money to the beggars on the street. I see a flicker of you every day, here and there.

I try to instil a little bit of you in the things I do and the words I say.

I help my classmates with their homework. I help an old man cross the street. I help my mother in the few ways I can think of.

But as I grow up, I notice something that disturbs me. As times change, you come with a price. At least that's what everyone around me tells me. They sneer at me and mock my tendency to help. I hear my elders telling me the world is cruel and I'd be trampled down like a delicate flower if I keep holding onto you. I hear my friends telling me about how I'll be taken for granted if I continue to be the way I am.

To be kind was often synonymous with being weak, miserable, pathetic, and gullible in modern jargon. It felt like doing the wrong thing by helping someone when I felt all piercing eyes on me, judging me, and taunting me. And today as I look around, I see people, malice coating their voices, selfishness guiding their actions, and their eyes filled with malevolence. I've heard poets talk of how the apocalypse will be a human's own doing, of how actions guided by inconsiderate motives will lead this world to its doomsday. I've always brushed those theories off, saying the poets merely needed inspiration.

But now every time I see someone doing something nice, the world seems to want to teach them a lesson merely for being selfless. I see humanity burn down to levels beyond repair. And yet, amidst these burnt ashes, flickers of hope flash here and there. I still see people helping one another, deciding against walking away. It gives me more than just hope; it lights a fire within me. A fire to speak against those who burn any and everyone who hinders their way to winning this corporate rat race.

A fire I hope never dies. You see, in a world that ours has become, all we're ever told by the people who apparently care for us is to look out for ourselves. To put ourselves before every other person, for otherwise, we'll lead ourselves to our own destruction. But in such a world, people who decide to help anyway are, in a way, a part of a rebellion. A rebellion against those who shamelessly call themselves humans yet walk around with no trace of humanity in their blood. A rebellion that may not involve public speeches and riots on the road, but a rebellion that manages to send across the powerful message just as fine. A message for the generations to come to live by.

And I promise not to become just another submissive servant of this system. I promise to succumb to this voice inside me that hums the songs of resistance, of the need to fight against cruelty, to fight for kindness.

Love,

Someone who will always fight for you

Dear Hope,

I know I have no business writing letters to you when I've let go of you more times than I can remember. But I want you to know that I don't mean to push you away and shun you out. I just like to believe the people who say, "Expect disappointment, and you'll never be disappointed."

Because of the few times I held on to you, fewer were the times you made yourself worth holding onto. But it's not your fault, and I know that. It's all in my head. Whatever is meant to be will be, and I know that.

I can't promise to always keep you close, but I promise to never blame you if what I wanted didn't happen. There are always more things to come, and more situations that will teach me that keeping you close means that in some corner of my heart, no matter how downhill things are, I believe that better things will happen. I see different people every day, some who keep you close because they've never been on the receiving end of the bad parts, some who choose to keep you close even though you have let them down, and a few who've let go of you once and for all. But I see an unmistakable glimmer of misery in the eyes of the last group of people; they've given up on life in general. I don't want to become them; I want to keep you next to me no matter how bad things are. Because although I've regretted deciding to keep you close, every time you were next to me, the joy I felt, the happiness that radiated through me is not easily replaceable.

So, for better or for worse, you're stuck with me, and I'm stuck with you. Because I've learned that blaming you for everything bad is the loophole that's got so many people stuck in this endless circle of pain and rue; you are not at fault. We are responsible for anything and everything life throws at us. Yes, I believe in fate, but that doesn't mean I'm going to transfer the blame to someone else for the consequences of my very own actions.

Here's to bad and good times, celebrations and mourning, loving and losing, and all other things that add colour to life.

Love,

Someone who wants to believe in you

Dear COVID,

You've become quite a popular public figure, haven't you? Everyone's been talking about you, a puny monster since March 25, 2020. I remember that date exactly because it was when my math exam was supposed to be held but got cancelled due to the lockdown.

So yes, my first few months of school got cancelled, and I got to productively use my first few months at home. After that, like all other sensible people in the world, I turned to Netflix for entertainment. And then you made it possible for me to sit at home—and by home, I mean anywhere at home: the couch, the bed, or even the bathroom—and attend classes. How? By looking at the screens of my gadget. Did I ever imagine that a day would come when I would have to eagerly wait to 'physically meet' my friends and teachers, when my teachers wouldn't have the choice to catch the boys talking or the girls gossiping? Now, at our service for our protection, is what they call 'the mute button.' Nope.

You made people tie the knot looking at their laptops. Because of you, 'Work from home' is no longer that popular song; it's a way of life. You promoted the 'common cold' from being an excuse for not wanting to do things to being a symptom of you—a life-taking virus.

But most of all, I see you spreading—not just as the virus but as the loss of humanity, of friendships, of hope. Every day, people die in numbers I do not wish to state. People have lost mothers, fathers, children, grandparents, friends, relatives. Do you not feel cruel and heartless? After all that you've done, you wish to come in newer and newer forms? They say you originated in China, but believe it or not, it's God's plan. He's playing a game, a game of trust; he's testing us all. He saw us not utilising the planet properly; he saw us wasting resources. He wanted us to prove ourselves worthy of living on Mother Earth.

He still does. He still feels we would take everything for granted once again if things get back to being normal. But ask him if you ever meet him—Why punish everybody? Ask him why innocents die every day. Ask him how it's fair for a little girl to become orphaned. Ask him for how much longer doctors must suffer, and ask him when it'll be over.

But also, thanks! Why? Because two years at home brought me closer to my family. It helped my brother, my mother, and me spend more time with my dad, who used to stay away from us before the lockdown. You helped me learn quite a few new things, and you offered me a relaxed, lazy lifestyle I got quite used to.

But no! None of this mellows down the crimes you've committed, none of this saves the lives you've taken. People usually end letters with warm quotes, but all I have to say to you is I'm happy you've slowly found your way out of our lives. It's a huge relief.

Wishing for you to never return,

Your forever enemy

Dear reader,

I'm the kind who's picky with her books; I will not just read anything given to me, not most times. I love experimenting, yes, but I know and understand the value of the time one devotes to reading a storybook amidst the other busy happenings in their life.

And so, I'd like to take one of these many random stories to tell you, thank you. Thank you for seeing life through my eyes as you flipped through these pages. Thank you for picking this book up and reaching all the way up here when you could have very well scrolled through your Instagram. Thank you for considering this book worthy of your time, money, and energy.

As an ardent reader myself, books fill me with the kind of joy that makes gardens bloom, that makes children laugh; the kind of joy that radiates from me to you and from you to the person right next to you. It all started with my first copy of a Famous Five book, and today I've come a long way with books but have remembered to keep them by my side every step of the journey. When it comes to role models, the first few people to cross my mind include authors like Rick Riordan or Khaled Hosseini, and Taylor Swift is a constant.

What I mean to say is books have a huge impact on my life, and reading is a hobby I love more than life. So, the fact that I've managed to whip up something that will be printed in pages and land up in your hands, and the fact that you might take the time to flip through numerous pages of me trying my hand at writing means a lot to me. Writing is something I've tried to hold on to ever since I discovered I could write moderately okay things. I'm not much of a dancer or singer; the farthest from them both, I'm your speech or poetry girl at talent shows.

Thank you once again. Love,

An aspiring author

26

I WANT TO BE DEFINED
BY THE THINGS I LOVE

I've seen numerous people posting across the internet that loving oneself is not as easy as loving the people in your life. Every day, I see people setting reminders to love themselves.

They paste sticky notes on the wall and write it down in their journal, thinking it will help.

I've personally always believed that it is because giving comes naturally to the human body. With no attached guilt or discomfort, you give endlessly. It is the easiest thing to do, to look at someone and decide that they're nice and fun. You consider yourself lucky for their presence in your life. You love them against all odds, for all their good and their bad.

I believe humans have an inherent quality to find a balance between the love they give and receive. They try to compensate for the lack of love they receive by giving out more and more. On the inside, we only hope and hope to be on the receiving end of love, but we cover it in a façade we call 'Selflessness' because will it not be embarrassing to confess you're desperate for love? Anyone who is afraid of love has succumbed to the intensity of it only to be failed, to be betrayed. And then there are some, the proud and the arrogant who believe no one can love as beautifully as they do. We talk of giving and receiving love like it must be weighed on a machine. We're all stuck in a loop of an ocean of overwhelming emotions.

But dear reader, you must understand that you get to learn as much about love from both its abundance and its absence.

When it comes to loving yourself, you're trying to discover a new person you only know through other people's eyes. You know yourself based on what they tell you about yourself, what they expect you to be, and what you've been defined as by them. Which is why you find it difficult to give yourself second chances, to learn from the mistakes you make instead of blaming yourself, and to forgive yourself for the few wrong decisions you make. I think I understand why people need constant reminders. It's because self-love isn't natural. It's not what we've been taught to do, what's been instilled in our minds since birth. It's difficult, you know, finding a perspective as kind as yours. Finding someone who'll truly define you for all the beautiful things you are.

Which is why we must take it upon ourselves to do that. Until we learn to do that, we can rely on these daily reminders. But I firmly believe that all of us will have that day in life when our eyes finally become capable of regarding us for who we are.

And I also believe that you are not defined by how you look. You're defined by the people who surround you. You're defined by the music you listen to, the shows you watch. You're defined by the things you do. You're defined by the art you create. You're defined by the kind of energy you spread.

So, I hope you find people who suffer from the same mental illness as you; they're the best kind! The kind who let you be real. You could tell them something weird, and they'll reply with something that's 10 times weirder. They'll know when you're not feeling too well, and they'll find the exact words to crack you up. Don't let go of them because they'll let you be goofy, weird, and all things real with absolutely no judgement. That group of people is pretty rare, so if you find one of those, you had better learn to value them. You'll like yourself better when you're around them, and that's a feeling you should hold on to.

I'm pretty sure that when you reach your grave, no one's going to remember the flab on your stomach or the pimple on your nose. The freckles on your cheek do not mean anything to the people who love you. You are not what your body makes you out to be; you are what you love. And if you are judged and called out by someone for looking 'ugly,' that someone needs to be kicked out of your life immediately. Because I don't think anyone is capable of looking ugly. If you love someone, they automatically look beautiful to you. So, it's probably not you; it's probably just the people around you.

And so, let this random note in this book serve as your daily reminder to maybe, for once, put yourself first. So, the next time you stare at the mirror, picking yourself apart, counting your flaws, I hope you see the beauty that lies in each blemish. You're not the scars on your skin but the shine that radiates through them.

It's a long road ahead, but it's part of the huge journey that will lead you up to where you've always wanted to be, to where you belong. Some days you'll feel lost and hopeless; some days you'll tread difficult pathways, and some days the prettiest of things will seem dull to you. But I hope on those days you remember to look at how far you've come. Every time you stare at a sky with no stars, I hope the ones that shine in your eyes are enough to brighten you up.

"I want to be defined by the things that I love.

Not the things I hate.

Not the things that I'm afraid of.

Not the things that haunt me in the middle of the night.

I just think that you are what you love"

Acknowledgements

I'd like to thank almost everyone and everything on the planet, from the shooting star I once wished upon to the lovely people in my life; they're all cumulatively the reason my name is on the freaking spine of a book.

Above everything, I'd like to thank God for giving me a happy and healthy life full of people I can always count on. I've had it better than a whole lot of people, and for that, I am forever grateful.

Thank you, dear reader. (Bonus points if you thought of the Taylor Swift song.)

But seriously, the fact that you decided to pick this book out of the millions that exist means a whole lot to me. I am forever grateful. Whoever is perusing this page right now, you're a huge part of this book-dream of mine come true, and I'm thankful from the bottom of my heart.

To my wonderful mother, thank you for letting me be a voracious reader and teaching me to devour books with all my heart. Your faith in me, your criticism, and your support are more than half the reason this book is not just a silly stupid idea.

To my amazing father, thank you for believing in me no matter what and being the hugest pillar of support. And an even bigger thanks for all the books you agreed to buy me; without them, heaven knows I would've never been able to write a whole book.

To my naughty, silly, and cranky brother, Shravan, you've inspired the book in more ways than one, and I'll never say it to your face, but yes, life without you would be less colourful. Just a little.

To my two awesome English teachers, Mrs. Priya Anna Thomas and Mrs. Mary Cyril, thank you so much for letting my ten-year-old self annoy you as much as she did. I owe a huge part of my vocabulary and writing skills to both of you. Thanks a tonne.

To Mr. Nakiran, someone I've had the joy of knowing since I was a little kid, thank you for fostering my interest in reading books and being a huge part of my journey as a writer. Without you, this wouldn't have been possible.

To my incredible cousin sister, Abhirami, thank you for taking the time to read the book and for your valuable criticism. I have always been in awe of your writings, and they continue to inspire me more and more every day.

To another one of my amazing cousin sisters, Ananya, thank you so much for being so encouraging about the book. Your compliments and criticism played a huge part in the finishing of this book, and for that, I am forever grateful.

To my awesome aunt, Mrs. Uma Krishnan, who once again continues to inspire me more and more every day, thank you so much.

To my sarcastic-in-the-middle-name, most supportive, and harshest critique title-winning best friend, Diya Sarah, I love you to the moon and to Saturn. The fact that you took so much time to read this book with so much intricacy and gave me the hugest feedback ever means so much to me. You know I'll ramble on if I could. I'm forever grateful that we somehow bumped into each other and decided we'd be okay with teasing and ranting to each other for the rest of our lives.

To another very good friend of mine, Risha Goel, thank you for taking the time to read through the book. It means a whole lot.

To every other encounter I've ever had in life, you must have somehow knowingly or unknowingly inspired this book, and I give you my hugest thanks for the same.

FROM THE READERS

Your work is brilliant, mature, and very reflective.

– Diya Sarah

It is simply superb. The language and the way it's presented are unbelievable. Too good.

– Priya Anna Thomas

The unsent letters are exclusive. Wonderfully written.

– Mary Cyril

Overall, it's a perfect book, Shrishti. It touched me.

– Abhirami Ramesh

Beautiful writing. The personifications and expressions for the simplest of experiences are very heartwarming.

– Ananya Karthik.